Scale Studies for Bass

Major Scales & Arpeggios

by Dino Monoxelos

1 2 3 4 5 6 7 8 9 0

Visit us on the Web at www.melbay.com — E-mail us at email@melbay.com

Table of Contents

About The Author

I first want to dedicate this book to my Mom and Dad. If it weren't for your unconditional love and support, this book and all the other accomplishments in my life would have never happened!!!

Thank You!

Originally from the Boston area, Dino Monoxelos has been a professional bass player since he graduated high school (quite some time ago). He's an endorsing artist/clinician for Ampeg, Warwick Basses, and Dean Markley Strings as well as Product Specialist for Ampeg. He's toured with a number of different artists and bands all over the world. He is a graduate of Musicians' Institute and has studied with the likes of Steve Bailey, Gary Willis, Bob Magnusson, Jeff Berlin, Tim Bogert, Jim Lacefield, and Todd Johnson to name just a few. After graduating from MI, Dino began teaching there where he developed his own teaching and playing skills. After seven years of playing and teaching in Los Angeles, Dino has since moved back to his hometown of Boston, MA where he lives with his wife Rachel and daughters Samantha and Nicole. He maintains a very busy playing and teaching schedule as well as conducting clinics for Ampeg all over the country.

I would also like to thank all of the following people as well.

My wife Rachel and daughters Sami and Niki, the entire Monoxelos/Sancartier clan, Mom and Dad Doucette & the entire Doucette clan, Dana Teague and Michael Brown and everyone at Dana B. Goods/Warwick Basses, Bill Norton and Tommy Wilson and everyone at Ampeg, William Bay, Doug Witherspoon, Mig Gianino and everyone at Mel Bay Publications, Mica and Susan Wickersham at Alembic Basses, Dave Leinhardt at Dean Markley Strings, Dave Avenius, Dave Boonshoft, PJ and everyone at Aguilar, Frankie A.,Tim Bogert, Ray Brinker, Gary Hess, The Leslie Family, Evan Goodrow and the EGB, Carl Ayotte, Demetrius Spaneas, Jim Zaroulis, Mike Valeras, Eddie Jean, Steve Bailey, Todd Johnson, Tim Miller, everyone at Musicians Institute, Bruce Gertz, Rich Appleman, everyone in the Berklee bass dept., FZ, my brothers in crime; Dale Titus & Albie Dunbar.

Introduction

The purpose of this book is for two reasons actually. The first is to show the student the many different locations of each major scale and their patterns along the fingerboard, in one octave, two octaves and in complete forms in each location (position).

By learning the major scales and their patterns, you have no choice but to learn all the notes on the fingerboard. This just happens by default. Once you start to learn the scales, knowing where the notes are in relation to one another comes real easy.

If you follow this book, you will be able to play one octave, two octave, and be able to connect complete major scales up and down the fingerboard.

If you have a teacher, work with him/her on this book. If you are learning this on your own, you should be able to get through this book with no problem at all. I do have to say though that the help of a teacher is invaluable.

This book of Major scales is of course just one small aspect of playing bass but as a teacher of 15 years I feel that this is a very important starting point for any player at any level!

The way this book works is that it is broken down into several sections. Each section containing the fingering diagram of the fretboard and the written music as it appears on the staff along with the fingerings.

The first section focuses on one octave major scales and arpeggios in all twelve keys. Showing all the locations on the neck for each one octave major scale and arpeggio.

The next section shows all of the notes above and below each major scale and arpeggio in each position that you just learned in the one octave major section.

The last section shows all the notes above and below each major scale and arpeggio on each single string.

If you follow each section's lesson by playing and practicing the notes and the suggested fingerings, you will be on your way to being a fretboard master. Just think about what it would be like to connect any major scale or arpeggio up and down the entire fingerboard without any hesitation.

Practice these lessons diligently and meticulously and remember, start off slow and learn them right the first time. Then as you get comfortable with them, only then can you start to build up the tempo.

The Major Scale

Every musician/student whether they are young or old, play piano, violin, oboe, guitar, and yes even the electric bass, have to start off by learning one of the most important yet easiest scales to learn. The MAJOR SCALE. What is a major scale? In fact, what is a scale, let alone a major scale????

A scale is a succession of notes that start on one note and either ascend or descend to another note. Some scales have only five notes in them, some have more. The most common scales have eight notes in them and start on one note, usually called the Root, and climb through the succession of notes or intervals if you will. Root, 2nd, 3rd, 4th, 5th, 6th, 7th and 8th. The 8th being the octave of the Root. A Major scale uses all of the major intervals. Root, Major 2nd, Major 3rd, Perfect 4th, Perfect 5th, Major 6th, Major 7th and Perfect Octave.

Let's say for instance we were to start on a C which would be the Root. We would play C Root, D Major 2nd, E Major 3rd, F Perfect 4th, G Perfect 5th, A Major 6th, B Major 7th, and then C Perfect 8th or Octave. CONGRATULATIONS!!!!! You just played a C Major scale!!!!!

A Major scale can also be looked at as being made up of intervals or combinations of whole and half steps. Remember, a half step is the equivalent of one fret on your bass and a whole step is the equivalent of two frets on your bass. The half step/whole step formula for a major scale is as follows:

Whole Step, Whole Step, Half Step, Whole Step, Whole Step, Whole Step, Half Step

or

W - W - H - W - W - W - H

C D E F G A B C

So if you were to start this formula on any note on the bass and follow this formula, you will come up with a Major scale. Like we looked at earlier, start with C, go up a whole step and you come to D, from D go up another whole step and you come to E, from E go up a half step and you come to F, F to G is another whole step, G to A is another whole step, A to B is another whole step, and finally B to C makes up the final half step. Again, Congratulations!! You just played your second Major scale. Try doing this starting on other notes on your bass. You will find that by starting on other notes, you will have to play some notes either sharp or flat to accommodate the whole/ half step formula for the Major scale. This is why we have different keys and key signatures. If you try starting the Major scale formula on a G, you'll see that you have to make the Major 7th an F♯ to fulfill the formula.

You can do this exercise by starting on any given note, and following the formula up the one string you started on. You will end up on the same string one octave up.

One thing that you will notice throughout this book is how sometimes I'll refer to either a twenty-one fret or a twenty-four fret neck. Some of the patterns that you will see can only be done on a twenty-four fret neck. Does this mean that a twenty-one fret neck is inferior? Absolutely not!!! I just wanted to include all versions of a four string bass rather than leave notes out.

The whole idea of this book is to show you how you can play all of these Major scales in the many different positions along your fingerboard. By going through this book you will learn how to play one octave, two octave, and be able to connect Major scales up and down your fingerboard. This can only make you a better and more efficient player.

The sky's the limit, it's up to you to put the time into it!!!!!

The Circle of Fourths

The Circle of Fourths is basically a tool that helps the student to identify and be able to memorize all of the key signatures. The circle is split into two halves, the right half shows all of the flat keys, and the left half shows all of the sharp keys. The top of the circle starts off with the key of C Major, no sharps or flats. Then as you move to the right or clockwise, the next key on the circle is the key of F Major, a fourth up from C Major. The key of F Major shows one flat in the block beneath it, that one flat is B♭. Each time you move to the next block clockwise, you go up a Perfect 4th from the previous key. Each time you do this, you add one more flat to the key signature. Continue to do this all the way around the circle. When you get all the way around to the sharp keys, you start to subtract sharps from the key signatures. The other way to look at this is to go back to C Major and work your way down the sharp key side (counter-clockwise). Each time you move to the next key, add one more sharp to the key signature. This is why sometimes you will hear the Circle of Fourths referred to as the Circle or Cycle of Fifths. This simply means that the flat keys are now on the left side and the sharp keys are on the right side of the circle. This way here, when you go clockwise around the circle, now you are moving in intervals of fifths. In other words, C Major to G Major is a Perfect 5th, and then G Major to D Major is a Perfect 5th etc. As you go around the circle this way.

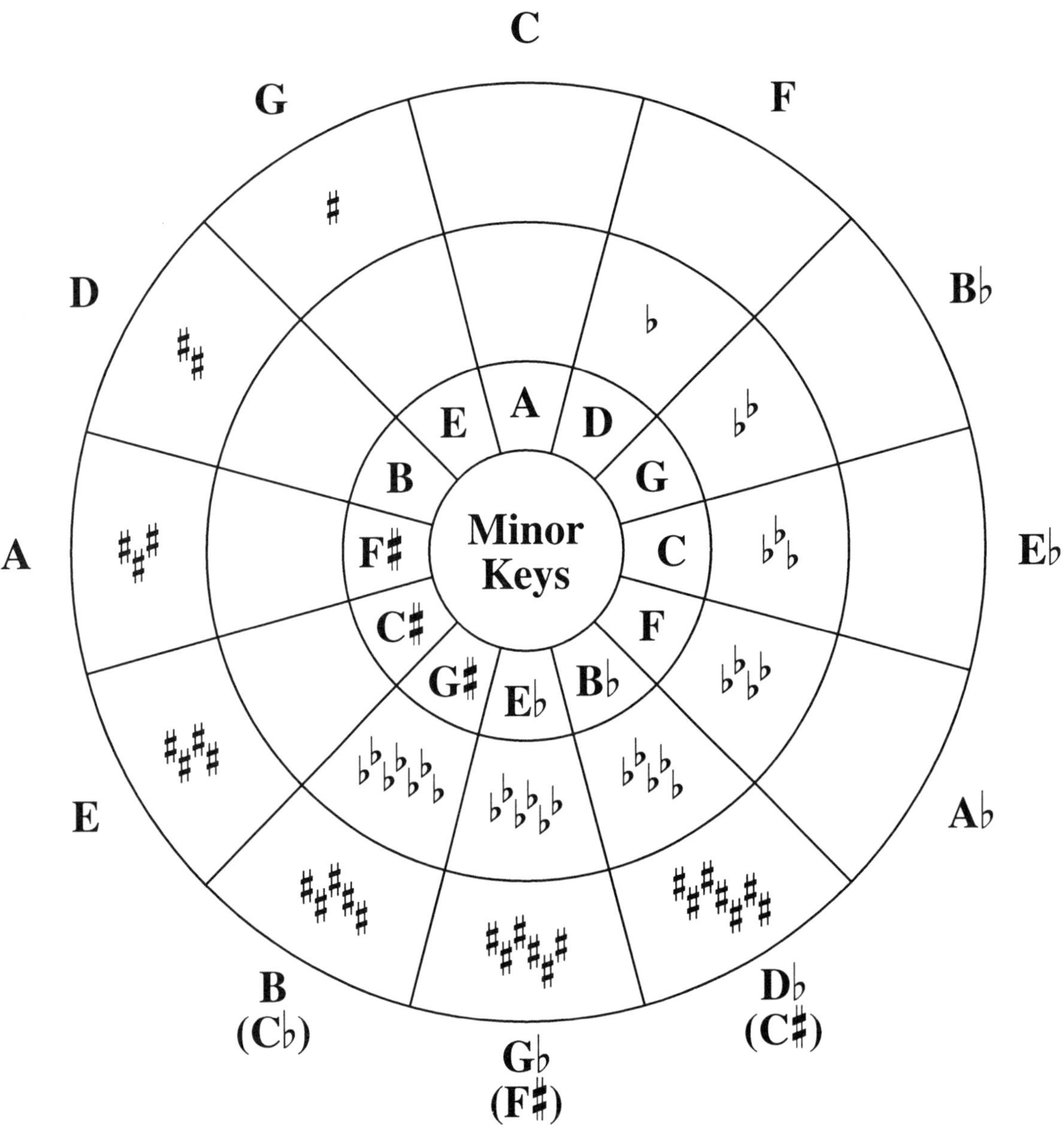

One Octave Major Scales

First thing that you should start with is the very basic, one octave, major scale. The easiest scale to learn first off is the C major scale because it contains no sharps or flats. As you advance in key signatures, you'll see the keys get progressively bigger and bigger, ie: more sharps and flats.

I set this book up so that as you look at each key, you will see the fingering diagram on the left page and the actual notation for the scale and the arpeggio on the right page. You will see that the first notated scale and arpeggio on the right page corresponds with the first fingering diagram on the left page.

As with most major scales on a four string bass, you will have at least three locations you can play the same fingering pattern up and down the octave. If you have a 24 fret bass, then you will have four locations in most keys.

Just make sure that you follow the fingerings that I've included because they are very important to knowing where each note is in relation to one another. Also, following these fingerings will promote proper left hand technique. Plus, as you progress in this book, you'll notice that you will be able to play in complete keys, in different locations on the neck, without having to move your hand all over the place. You're probably still asking, "so what is all that mumbo jumbo supposed to mean, I have a hard enough time just playing the notes as is", trust me on this, make sure you follow the fingerings. If you are taking lessons from a teacher, he or she will tell you the same thing.

C Major

①

Okay, let's take a look at C major. Example 1 starts us on C on our A string. We'll call this C-3-A. C on the 3rd fret on the A string. Follow the fingering and you'll see how the W-W-H-W-W-W-H formula works crossing strings. Now look at the corresponding scale and arpeggio and their fingerings. Notice where that first C is on the staff.

②

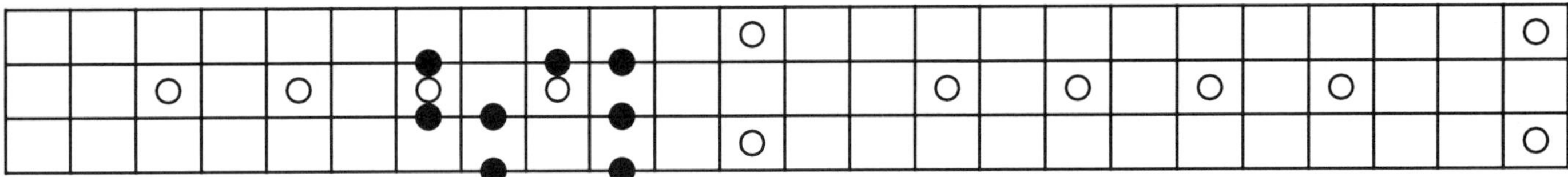

Now let's take a look at example 2. Now we start on C-8-E. Notice anything similar? The pattern is the exact same thing as in example 1. The only difference is that you are starting the same scale, only on a different location on the neck. Now look at the notation, it's also the same thing. That's because the notes ARE the same. Like I said, you're just playing them in a different location.

③

Take a look at example 3. This starts on C-15-A. What do you notice that's different. The C that you started on is actually the C that you ended on in the previous two examples. You are starting the scale one octave up. The pattern remains the same though. The only thing that changes is the notation. Now you are starting on the C above the staff which means you have to read the higher notes on ledger lines. You'll notice that in some examples I will write them with the ledger lines, and in other examples I'll write them in the lower octave with a 8va noted above the music. The 8va means to be played up one octave.

④

Example 4 takes you about as high as you want to go on the E string. C-20-E. If you have a standard 20 or 21 fret neck, you won't be able to use this example to it's fullest. If you have a 24 fret neck, you will be able to do this exercise however, you'll notice that that C starts to get pretty muddy sounding that far up the E string. It is important that you learn the surrounding notes though.

C Major

F Major

①

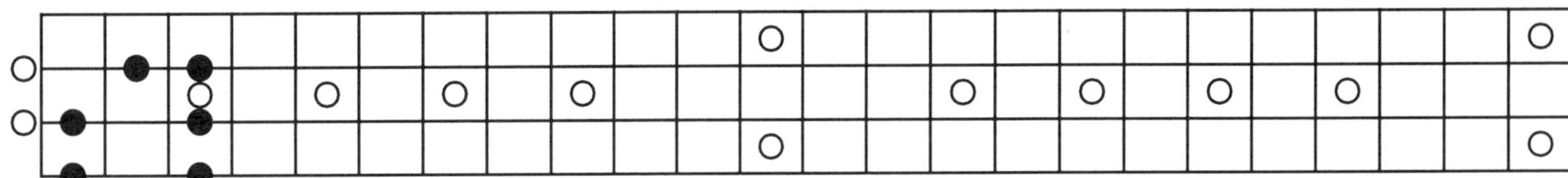

Now as we move around the Circle of Fourths, the next key we come to is F major. Now remember, if you follow the whole step / half step formula for a major scale, you'll see why F major has one flat which is B flat.

Let's look at example 1. The first F is F-1-E. You'll see that because of the position that you are playing this in, you can't use the same pattern that you are familiar with. You can take advantage of the open A and the open D string though. This is also the only F on your bass in that low register. Again, make sure to follow the fingerings I've included.

②

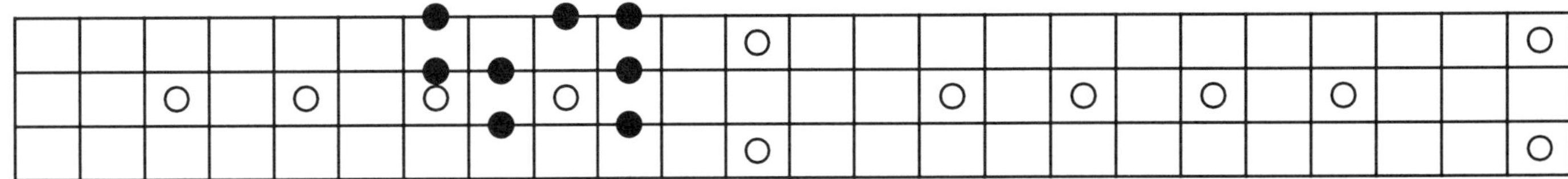

Now look at example 2. This one starts on F-8-A. Now you can go back to the same major scale pattern that you are familiar with. Again, be sure to follow the fingerings for both the scale and the arpeggio.

③

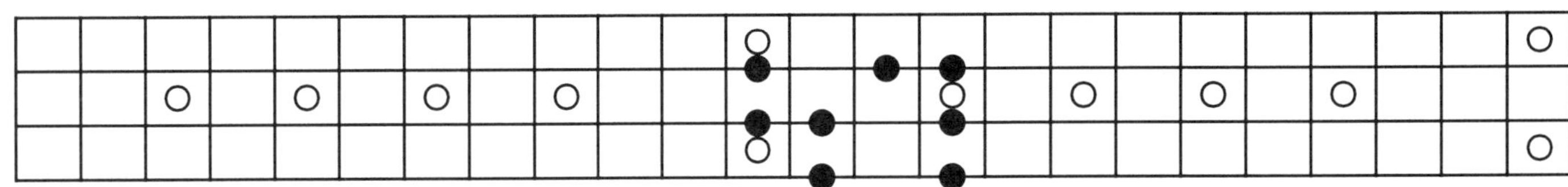

Example 3 now takes you to F-13-E. This is in the same register as the previous example just higher up on the E string. The pattern is the same though.

④

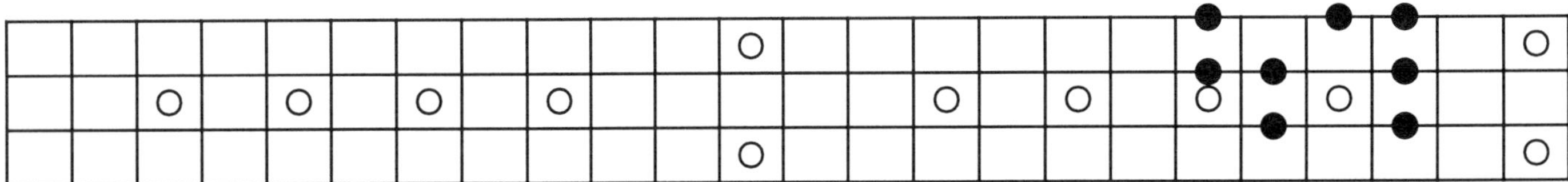

Now finally we go on to the last example. Again, this will only work if you have a 24 fret neck. If you have a 20 or a 21 fret neck, you will have a hard time getting to those notes that high up on the fingerboard. Look at the notation on the staff though. Remember how I said some examples would be written with ledger lines above the staff and some would be written in a lower register with an 8va above, this is one of those examples. The fingerings are still the same as the previous two examples as well.

F Major

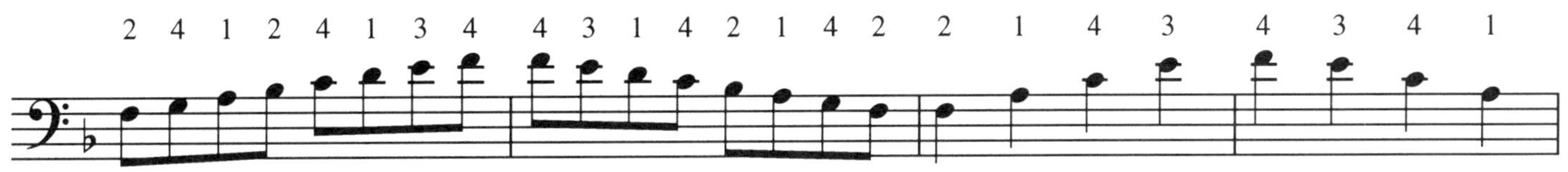

B♭ Major

①

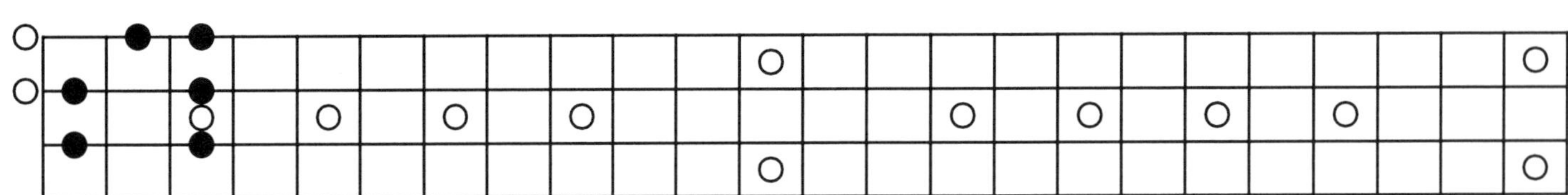

Next on the circle is B flat. Now here we add another flat so now we have B♭ and E♭. Example 1's fingering is going to be different because of the open string position. Be sure to follow the fingering and you'll be fine.

②

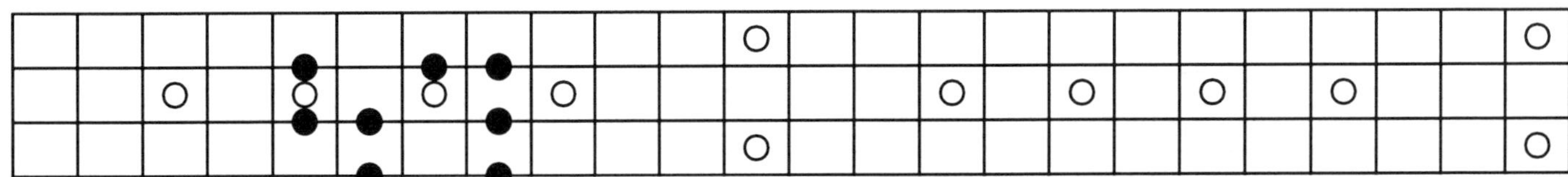

Examples 1 and 2 are in the same register so they will appear in the same place on the staff. Example 2 starts you off at B♭-6-E though. At this point you are back to your familiar pattern.

③

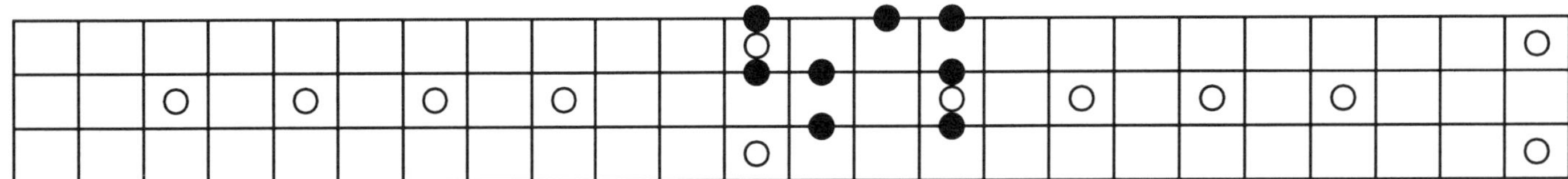

Examples 3 & 4 now take you to the higher octave. Remember, the B♭ that you are starting on is the B♭ that you ended on in examples 1 & 2.

④

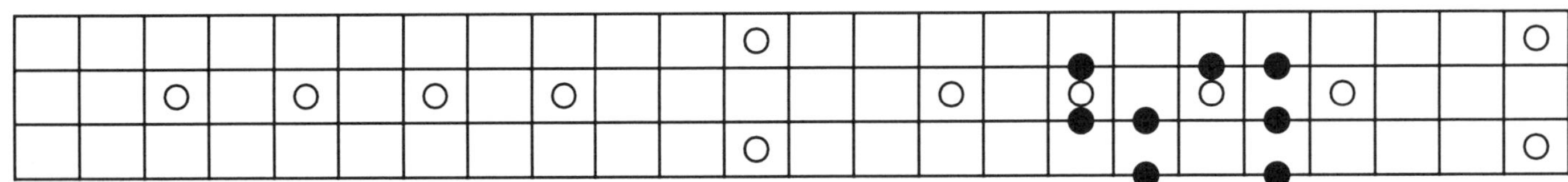

Example 3 starts you off at B♭-13-A where example 4 starts you at B♭-18-E. Again, watch out for those 20 and 21 fret necks.

B♭ Major

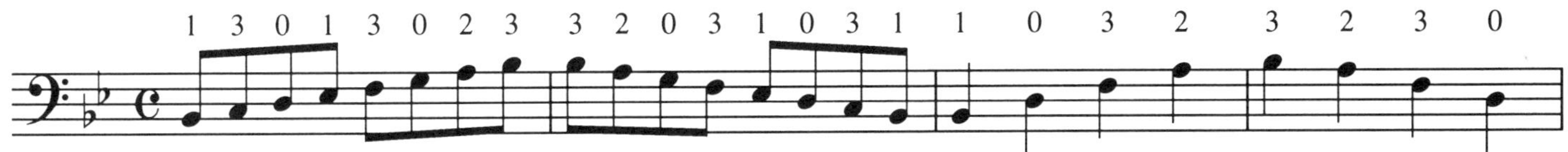

E♭ Major

Okay, next stop on the cycle is E♭ major. Let's add another flat which now gives us B♭, E♭ and A♭. Look at how high up the neck example 1 starts you at. You could start at E♭-1-D but you would have to make some fancy shifts to get up to the E♭ on your G string so I thought it would be best to start you off at E♭-6-A. You actually only have three examples in this key. Example 2 starts you off at E♭-11-E and example 3 starts you at E♭-18-A. You could start again at E♭-23-E but like I said before, this does you no good if you have a 21 fret neck. If you do have a 24 fret neck, you can attempt example 4, just be sure to follow the fingerings no matter how weird they get. I also included both the actual notation and the 8va notation on the notation page for examples 3 and 4.

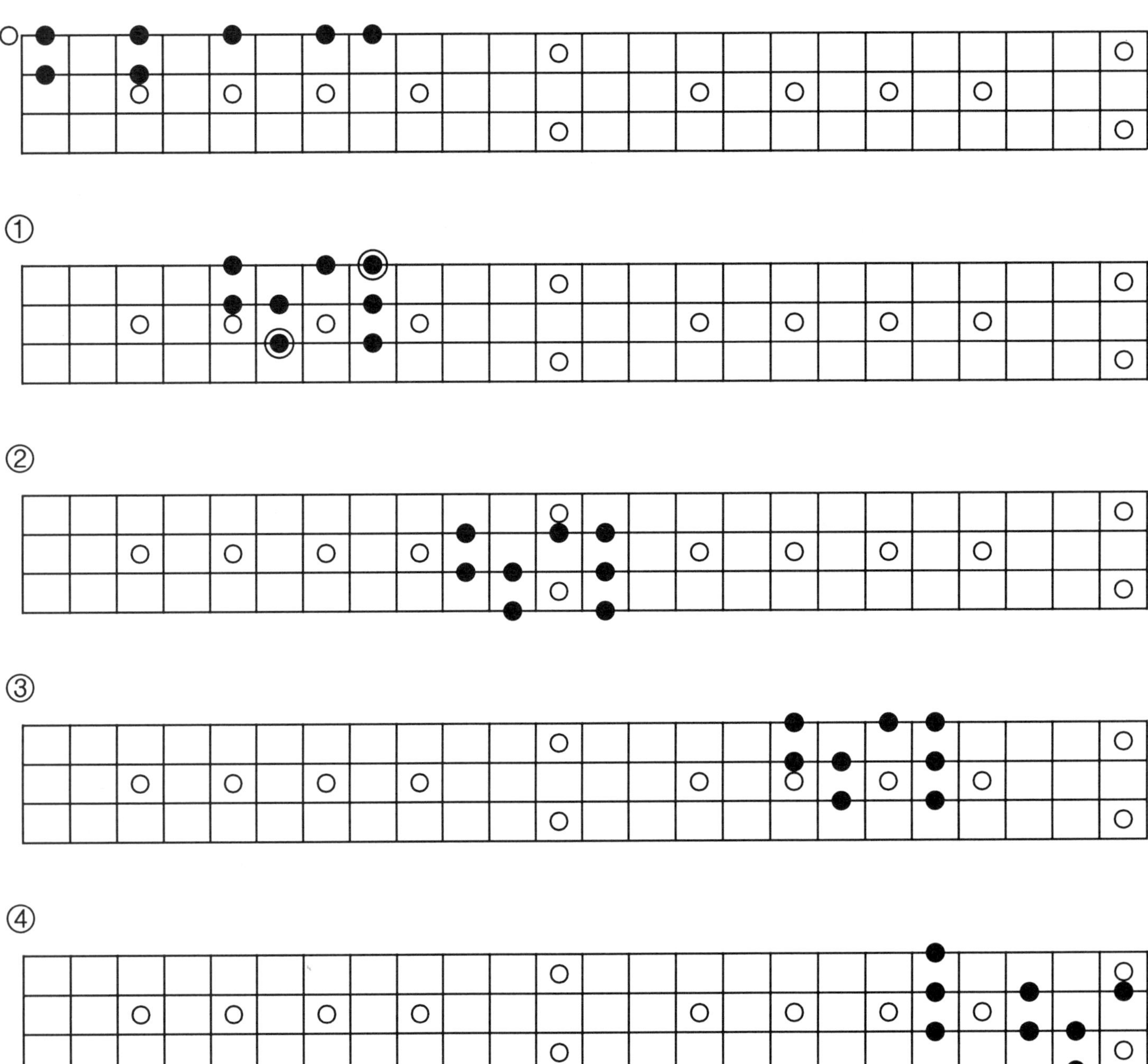

E♭ Major

A♭ Major

Next on the circle is A♭ major. Again, we add another flat so now we have B♭, E♭, A♭, D♭. Are you starting to see a pattern develop? Example 1 starts you at A♭-4-E. Again you are back to your familiar pattern. This A♭ is the only A♭ in this register on your bass. When you get to example 2, you are already up to the octave at A♭-11-A. Example 3 takes you to A♭-16-E. This is still in the same register as you see in example 2. You can do the same thing that you did with example 4 in the E♭ example. The only problem is that you will not be able to finish the scale because even a 24 fret neck only goes as high as G. You'll fall a half step short of the full scale. It is good to know that you have an A♭ at the 23rd fret though and that you can play most of the scale.

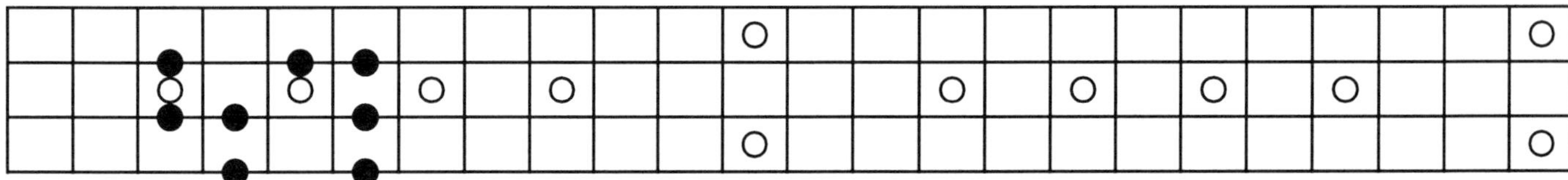

②

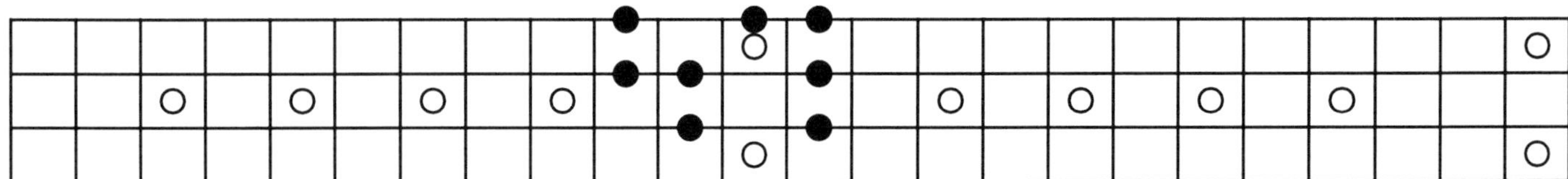

③

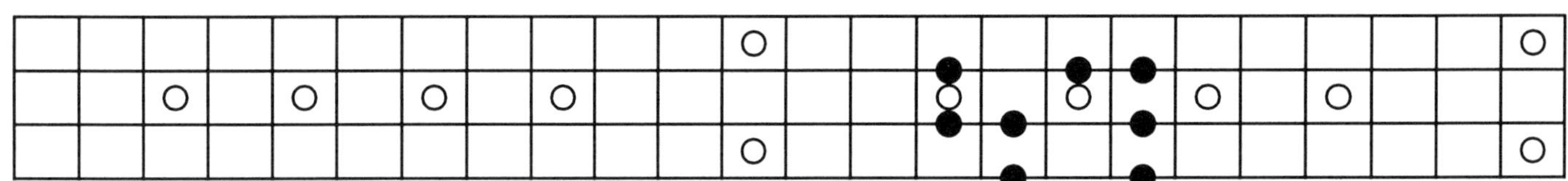

④

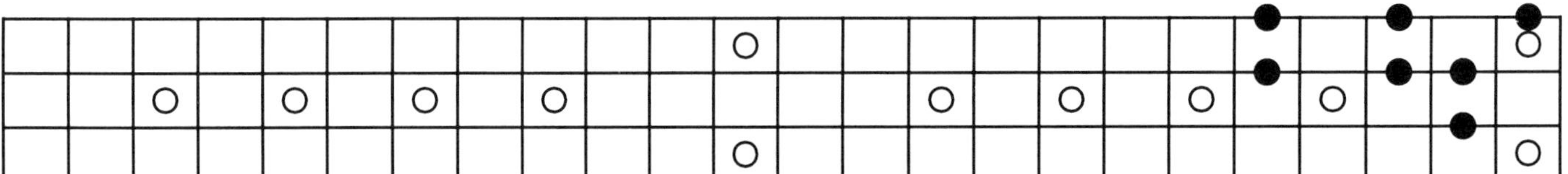

A♭ Major

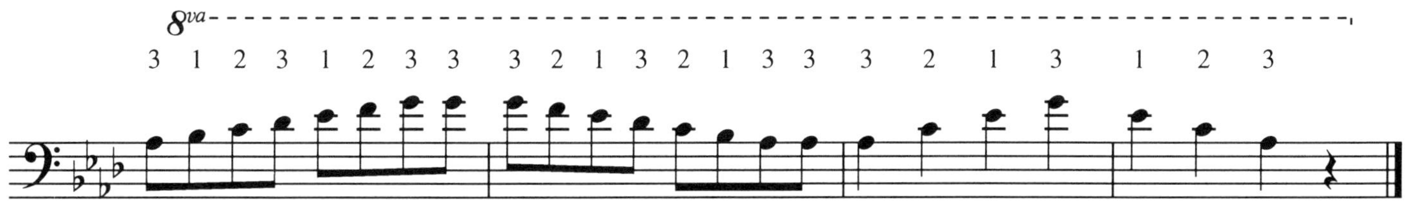

D♭/C♯ Major

I bet you're asking why this section has two names. Well because it does have two names actually. If you look at the patterns for D♭ and then look at the patterns for C♯, you'll see that the patterns are identical. You'll see the difference when you look at the notation on the opposite page. D♭ has five flats in it's key signature whereas C♯ has seven sharps. The actual notes are the same, what has changed is their names. When you are in D♭ you have D♭, E♭, F, G♭, A♭, B♭ and C; five flats. When you are in C♯ you have C♯, D♯, E♯, F♯, G♯, A♯ and B♯. It's much easier to keep track of five flats than it is to keep track of seven sharps, right!! So why have two names, why not just call it D♭? Well, you could however, this is what we call an enharmonic key meaning that it belongs to both the sharp keys and the flat keys as well, as you will see in the next few keys. Be sure to follow the fingerings and to help you along, say each note as you play it. Make sure not to mix the names of the notes from each key signature.

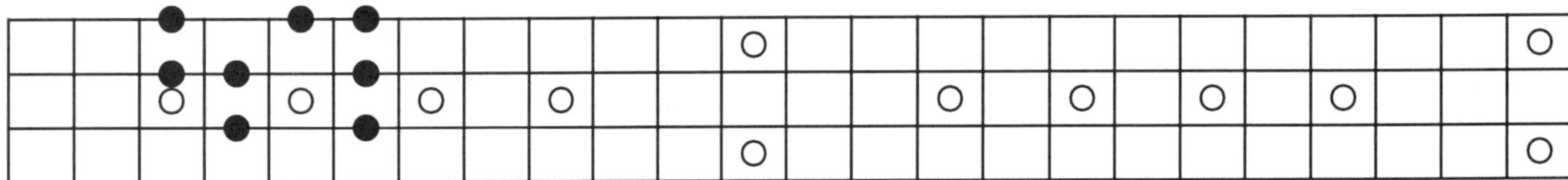

②

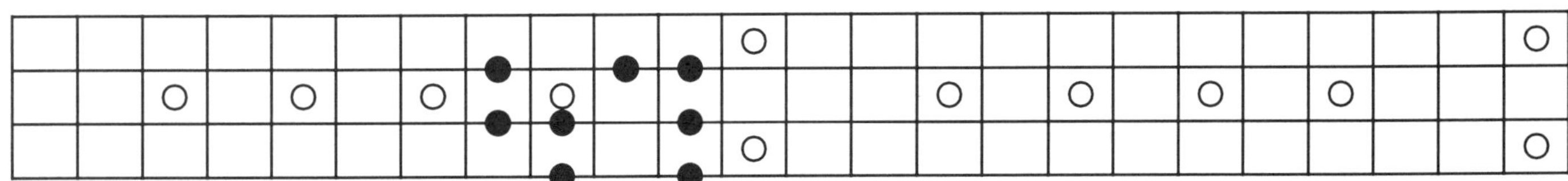

③

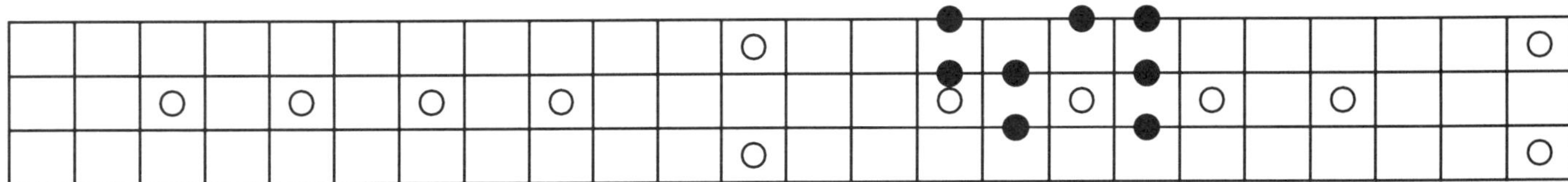

④

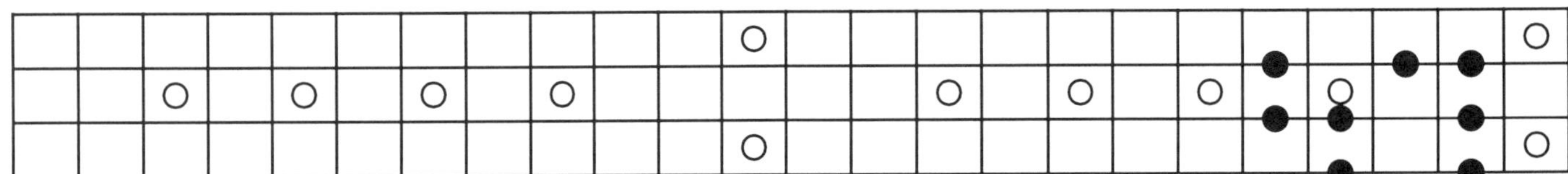

D♭ Major

C♯ Major

G♭/F♯ Major

Yet another one of those pesky enharmonic scales. Now we have G♭ major which contains six flats and F♯ major which contains six sharps. Now this really gets confusing. So which key is easier to use and why would I pick one key as opposed to the other. All great questions. At this point it's up to the player and or composer's discretion. If you are playing a piece of music that started out in the key of let's say F major and then modulated up a half step somewhere throughout the song, it might be better to say it's now in F♯ to restate that it modulated up one half step from the key of F major. Again, be sure to follow the fingerings and be sure to say the notes as you play them, especially when playing the arpeggios.

①

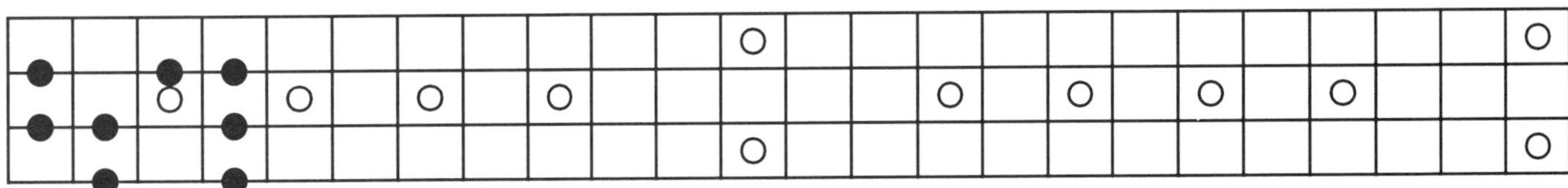

②

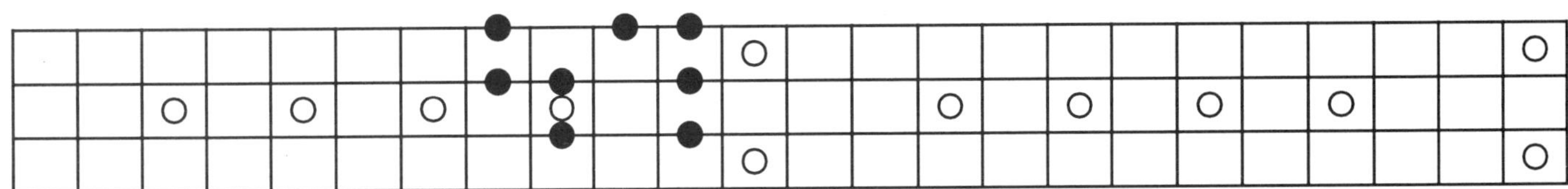

③

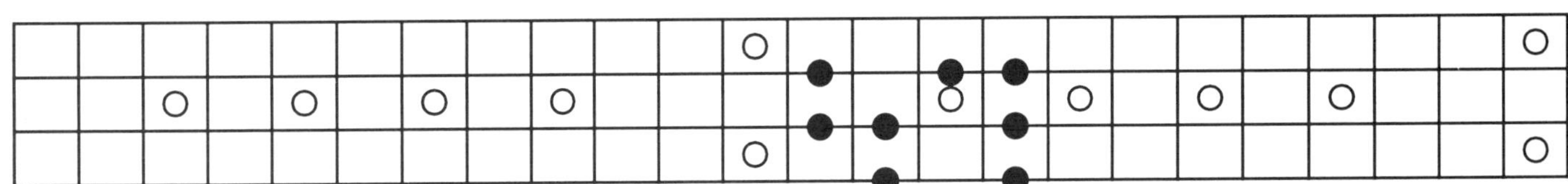

④

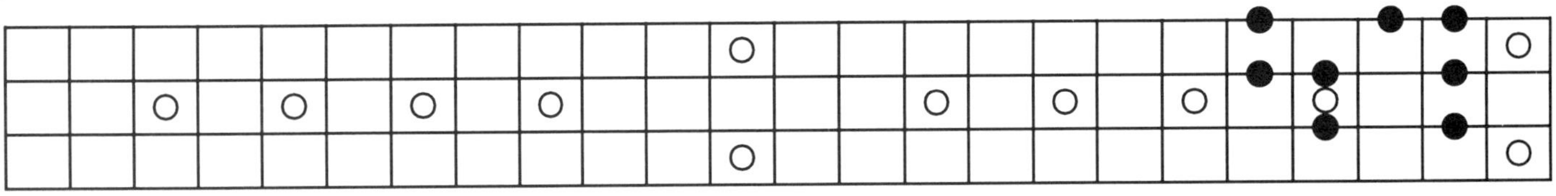

G♭ Major

2 4 1 2 4 1 3 4 4 3 1 4 2 1 4 2 2 1 4 3 4 3 4 1
2 4 1 2 4 1 3 4 4 3 1 4 2 1 4 2 2 1 4 3 4 3 4 1
2 4 1 2 4 1 3 4 4 3 1 4 2 1 4 2 2 1 4 3 4 3 4 1
2 4 1 2 4 1 3 4 4 3 1 4 2 1 4 2 2 1 4 3 4 3 4 1
F♯ Major
2 4 1 2 4 1 3 4 4 3 1 4 2 1 4 2 2 1 4 3 4 3 4 1
2 4 1 2 4 1 3 4 4 3 1 4 2 1 4 2 2 1 4 3 4 3 4 1
2 4 1 2 4 1 3 4 4 3 1 4 2 1 4 2 2 1 4 3 4 3 4 1
8va
2 4 1 2 4 1 3 4 4 3 1 4 2 1 4 2 2 1 4 3 4 3 1 4

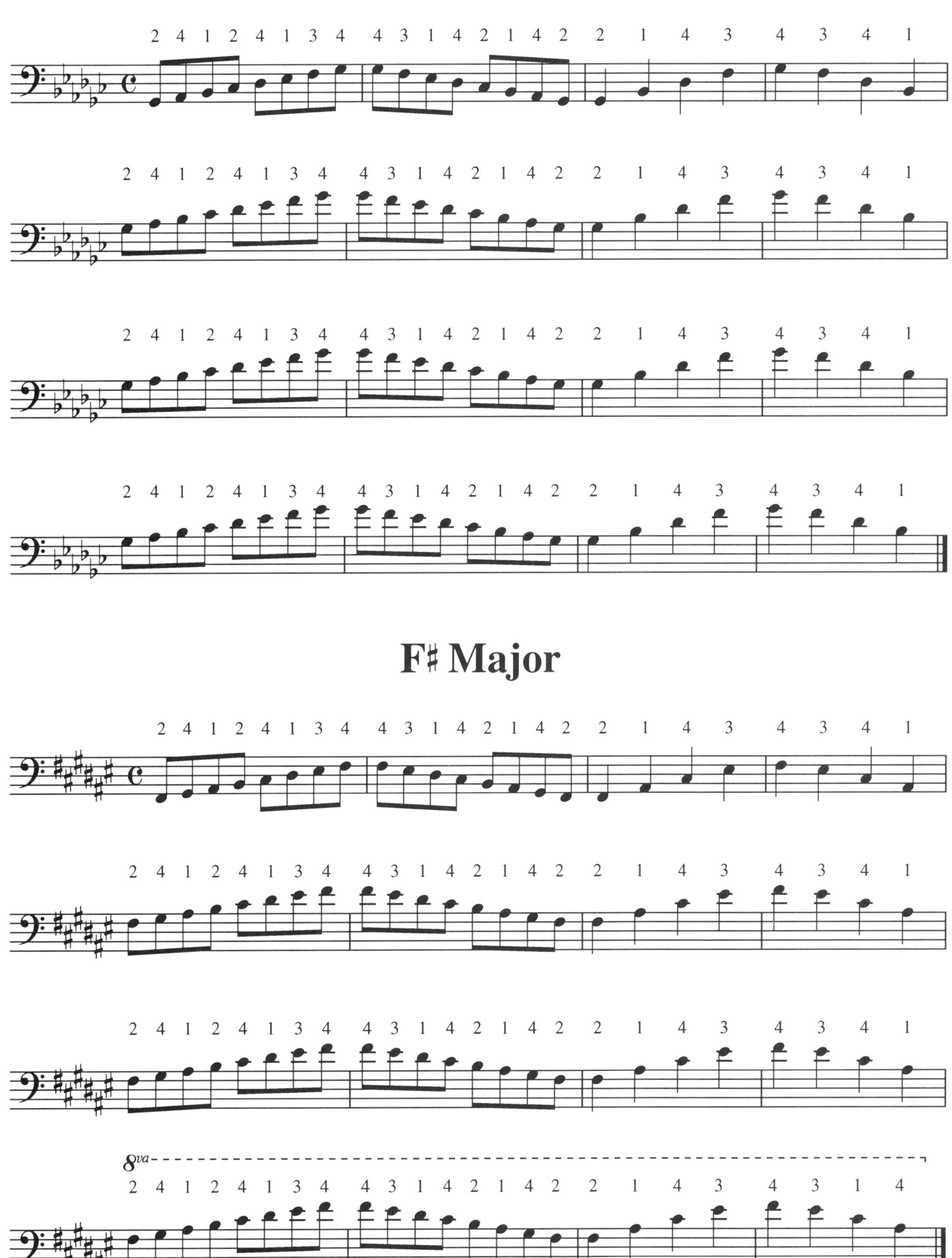

C♭/B Major

Now at this point the scales have tipped (no pun intended) in the way of the sharp keys. C♭ contains seven flats where B major contains only five sharps. Remember, the patterns are identical, the names of the notes are the only thing that has changed. Be sure to follow the fingerings in each of the four examples and make sure to say the notes as you play them.

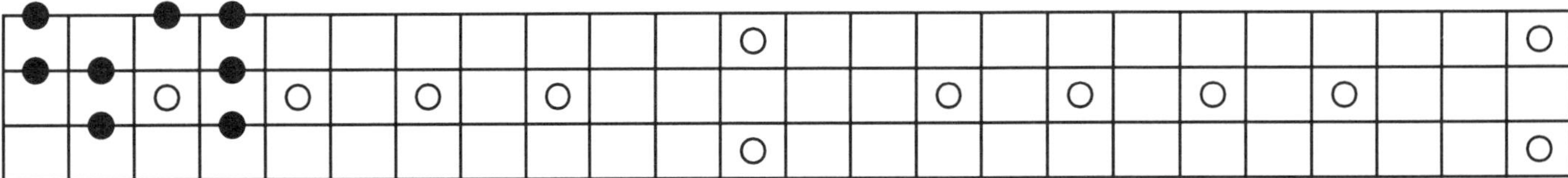

②

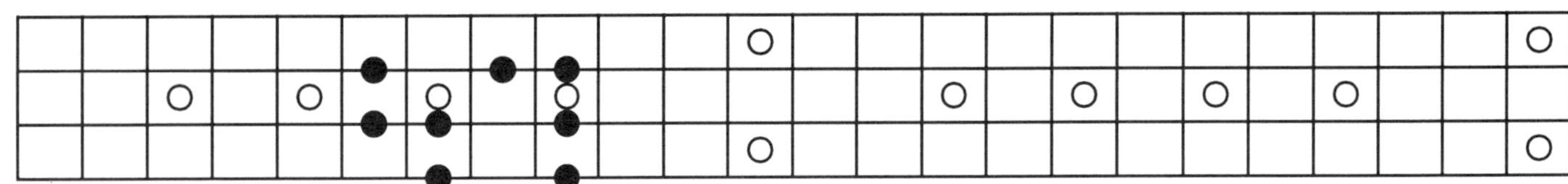

③

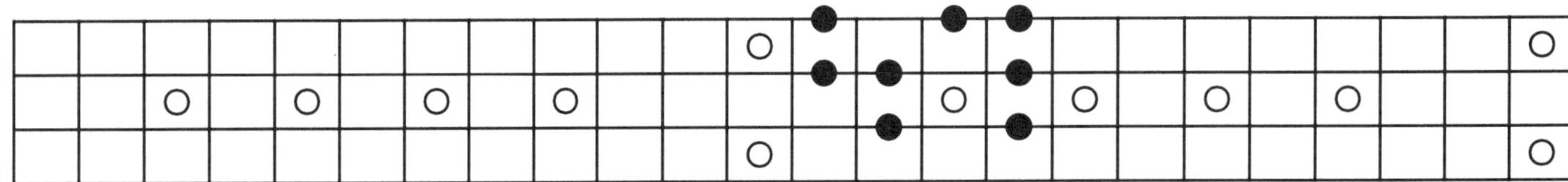

④

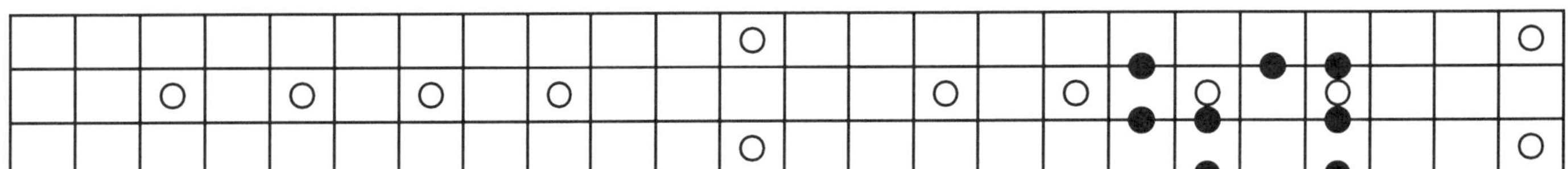

C♭ Major

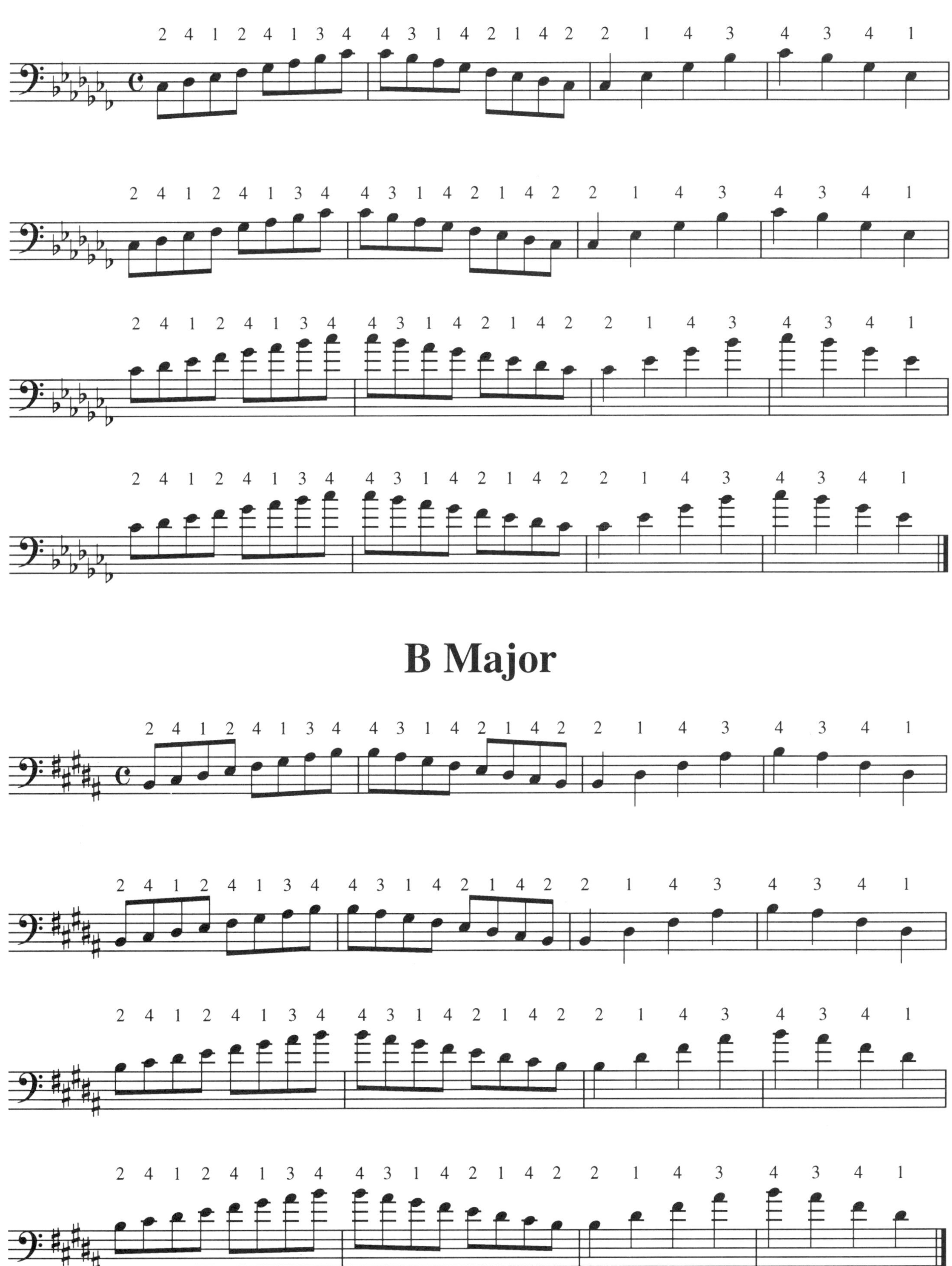

E Major

Now that we're out of the enharmonic keys, we can focus on coming back around to the top of the circle. This gets easier because as we get closer to the top, we actually start removing sharps as we progress through the keys. E major now only has 4 sharps in it's key signature. The first example starts you as low as you can go on a four string bass. This pattern forces you to use the open E and the open A strings. Be sure to use the fingering I've done. The remaining three examples are pretty straight forward as you should be a pro at this one octave major scale pattern by now!! Remember though, say it as you play it!!!

①

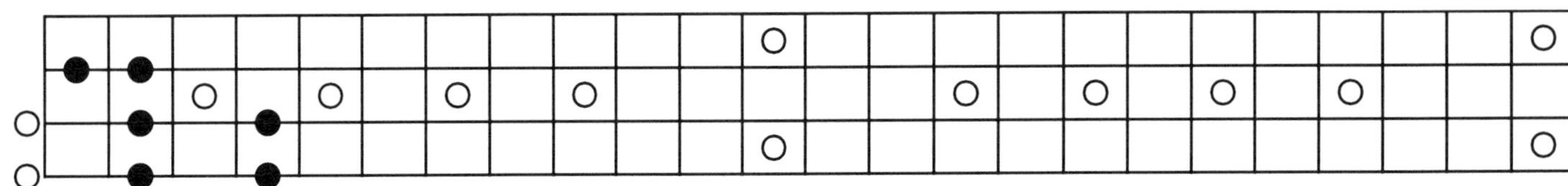

②

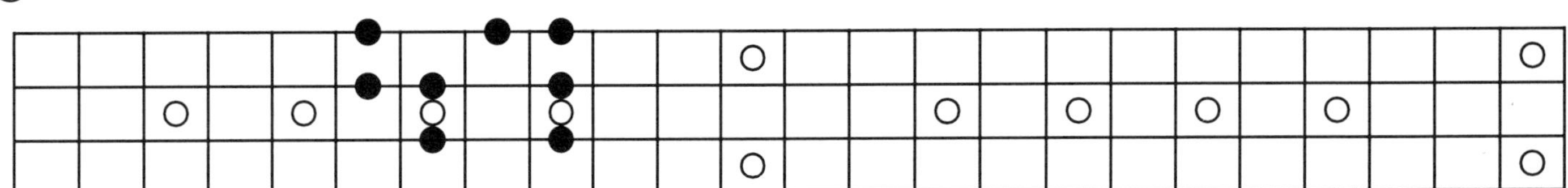

③

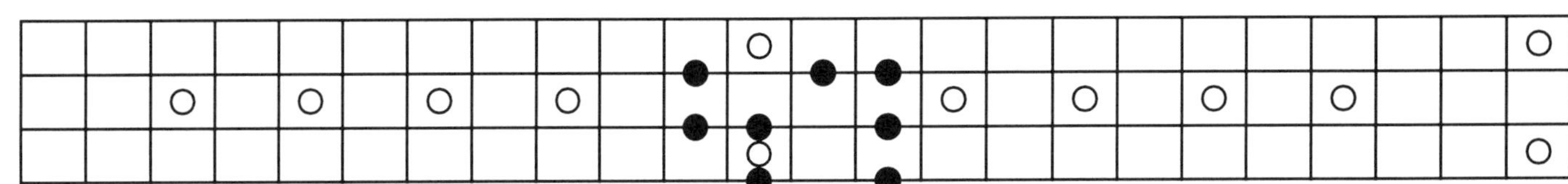

④

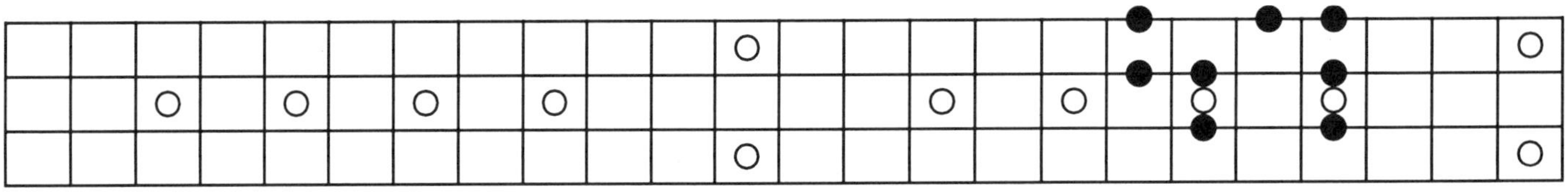

E Major

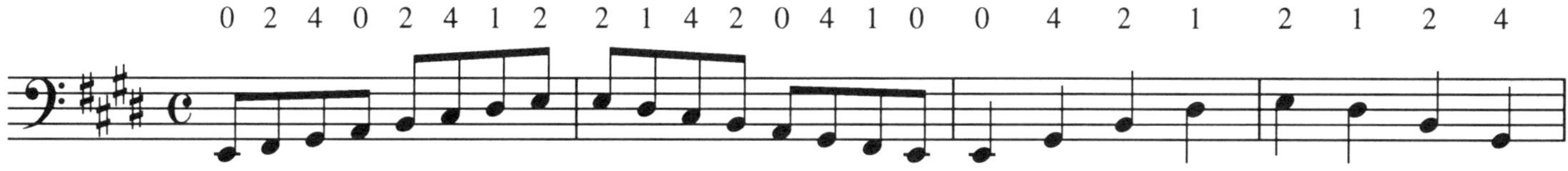

A Major

Like I had said, we start to remove sharps as we go through the sharp keys. A major now only has three sharps. Example 1 is similar to example 1 in E major, where you are forced to use the open strings. Follow my fingerings as you'll be okay. The remaining three examples are pretty straightforward as I've said. Remember that you do have one other A on the neck and that's at A-24-A. See if you can figure out the notes starting at that position. Once again, say it as you play it!!!

①

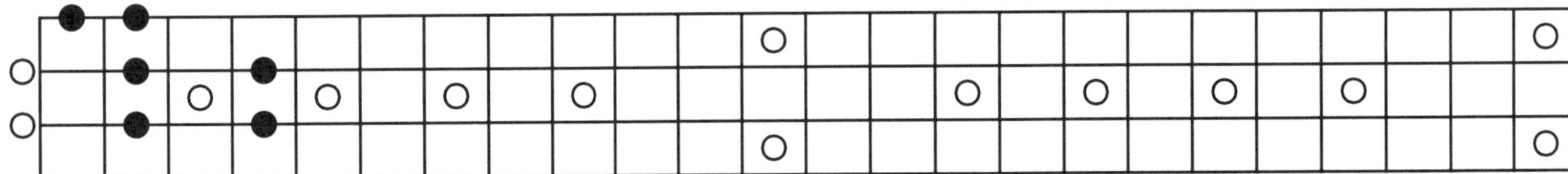

②

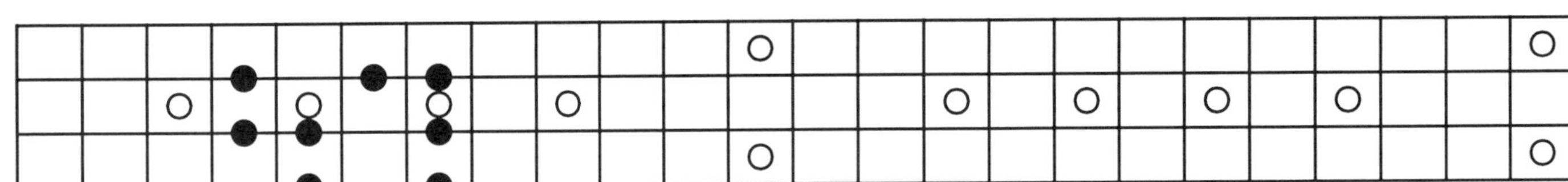

③

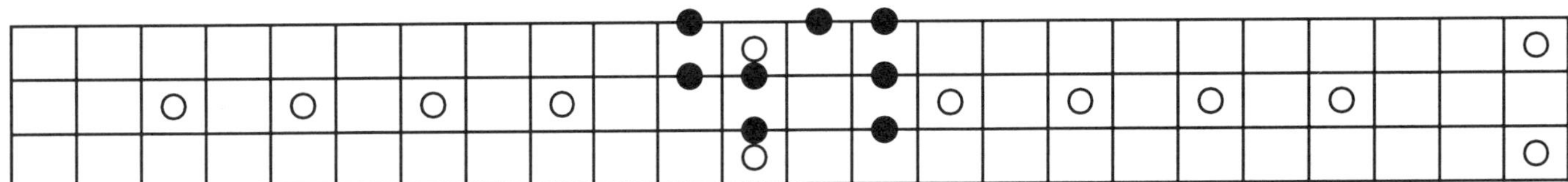

④

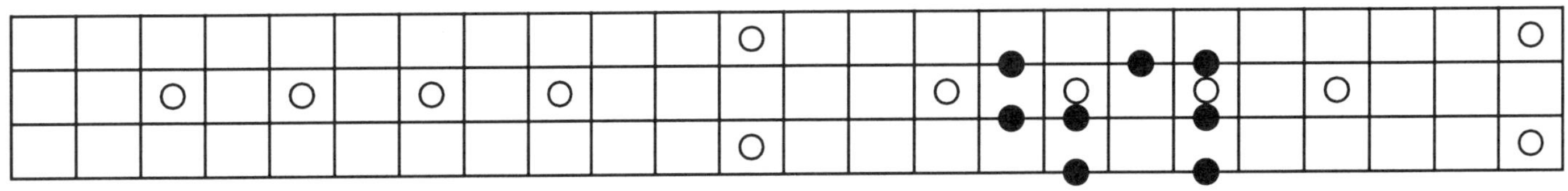

A Major

D Major

It gets even easier with D major. Now we have two sharps to contend with. These examples are very straightforward. You have two starting points in the lower registers. Example 1 starts at D-5-A, example 2 at D-10-E. And two starting points in the upper register, example 3 starts at D-17-A, and example 4 starts at D-22-E. Again, forget example 4 if you have a 21 fret neck.

①

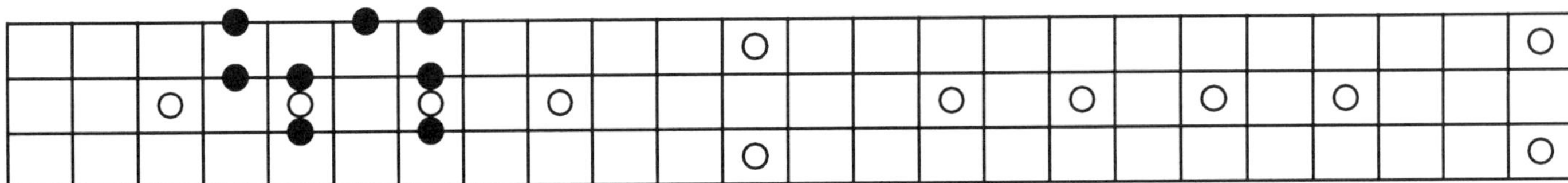

②

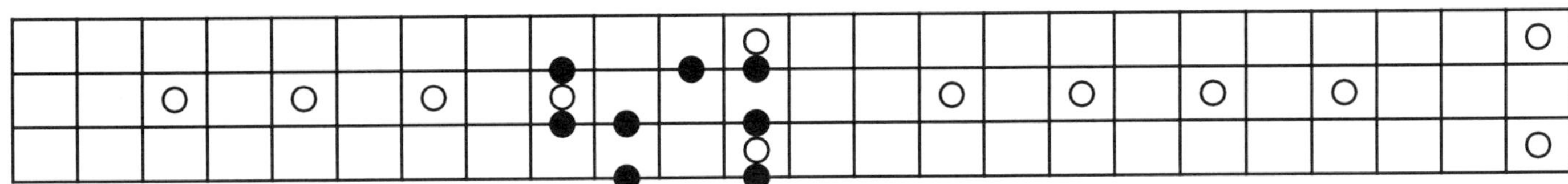

③

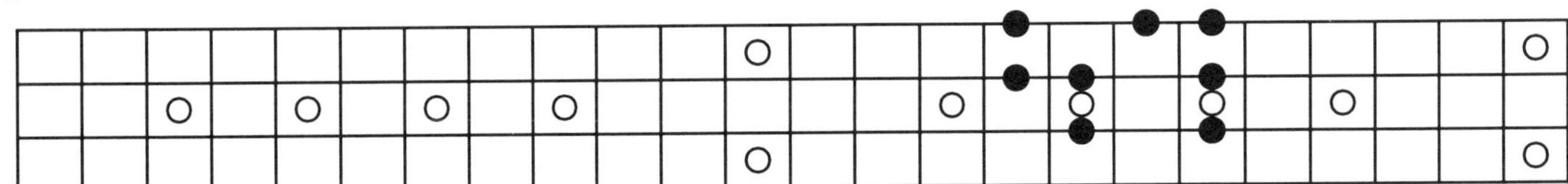

④

D Major

G Major

This is the easiest of the sharp keys, only one sharp to deal with, F♯. How easy can this get?!? Again, four patterns, example 1 in the lowest register; G-3-E, examples 2 & 3 starting in the middle; G-10-A and G-15-E, and example 4 starting an octave above those two; G-22-A. Remember, example 4 is only good for 24-fret necks.

①

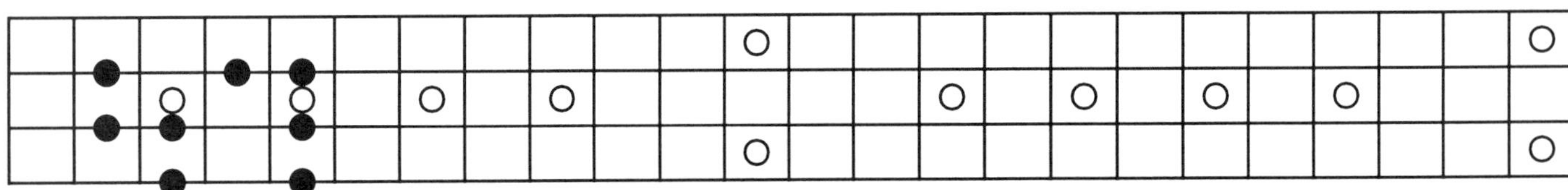

②

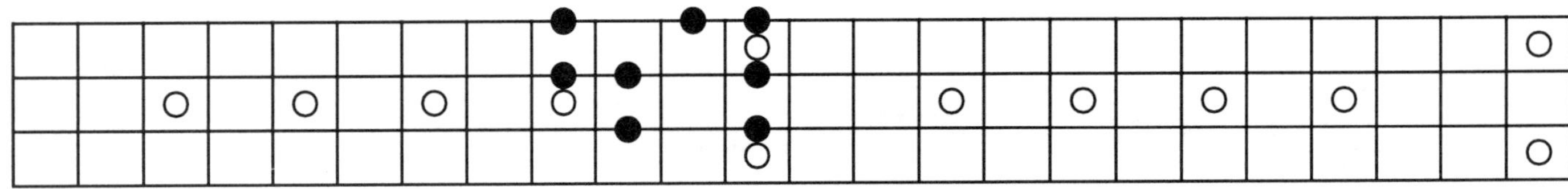

③

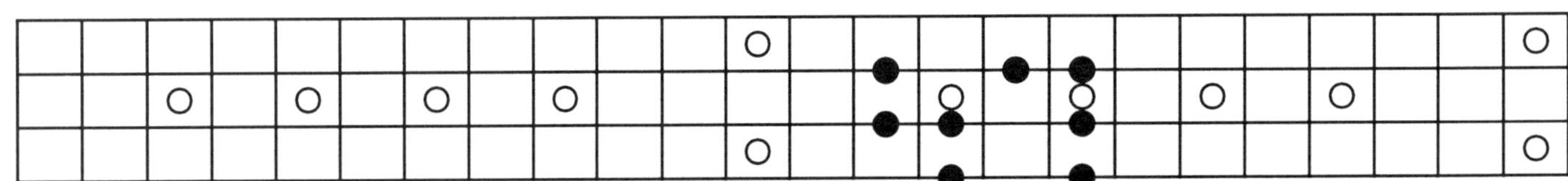

④

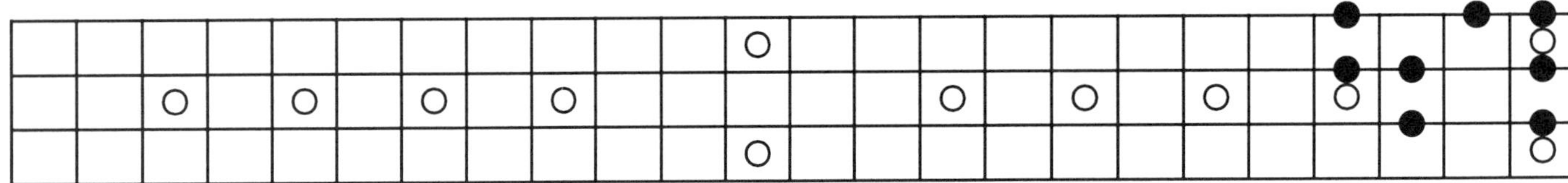

G Major

Full Position Patterns

C Major

Okay folks, now that you've gone through ALL of the One Octave Major Scales and One Octave Major Arpeggios, it's now time to take the One Octave Major Scale idea one step further. Now we're going to take each position that you learned for each major scale and build the notes of that scale *around* the root. In other words, take a look at the first C Major scale pattern. You will see the original C Major scale pattern but you will also see some notes that were added to the pattern, G-3-E and A-5-E. You could also add the F on the first fret as well as the open E. These added notes still belong to the C Major scale but they were added to the bottom of the scale as well. You learned the notes in the C Major scale, now you need to learn those notes throughout that entire position. This will help you to learn all of the notes in each major scale and arpeggio in each of the positions.

Play through each Major key. Play the arpeggio as well as the scale in each position and be sure to follow my suggested fingerings too. Start each scale and arpeggio slow and slowly build up the speed in which you can play them.

You will notice how some of the higher pitched scales are written in the actual ledger lines above the staff, and some of the scales are written one octave down with an 8va meaning to play it up an octave.

Good Luck and have fun with these and make some music!!!

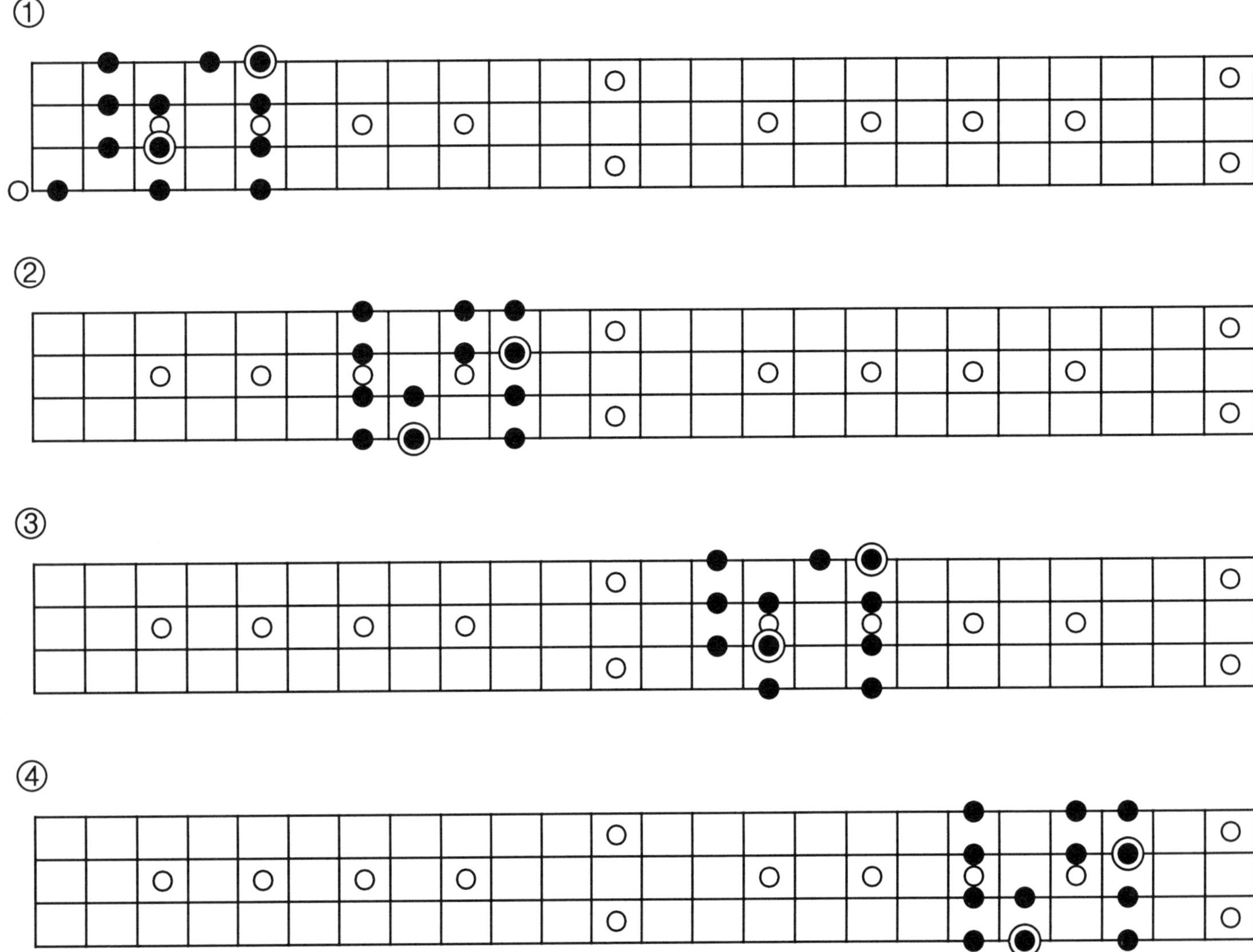

C Major

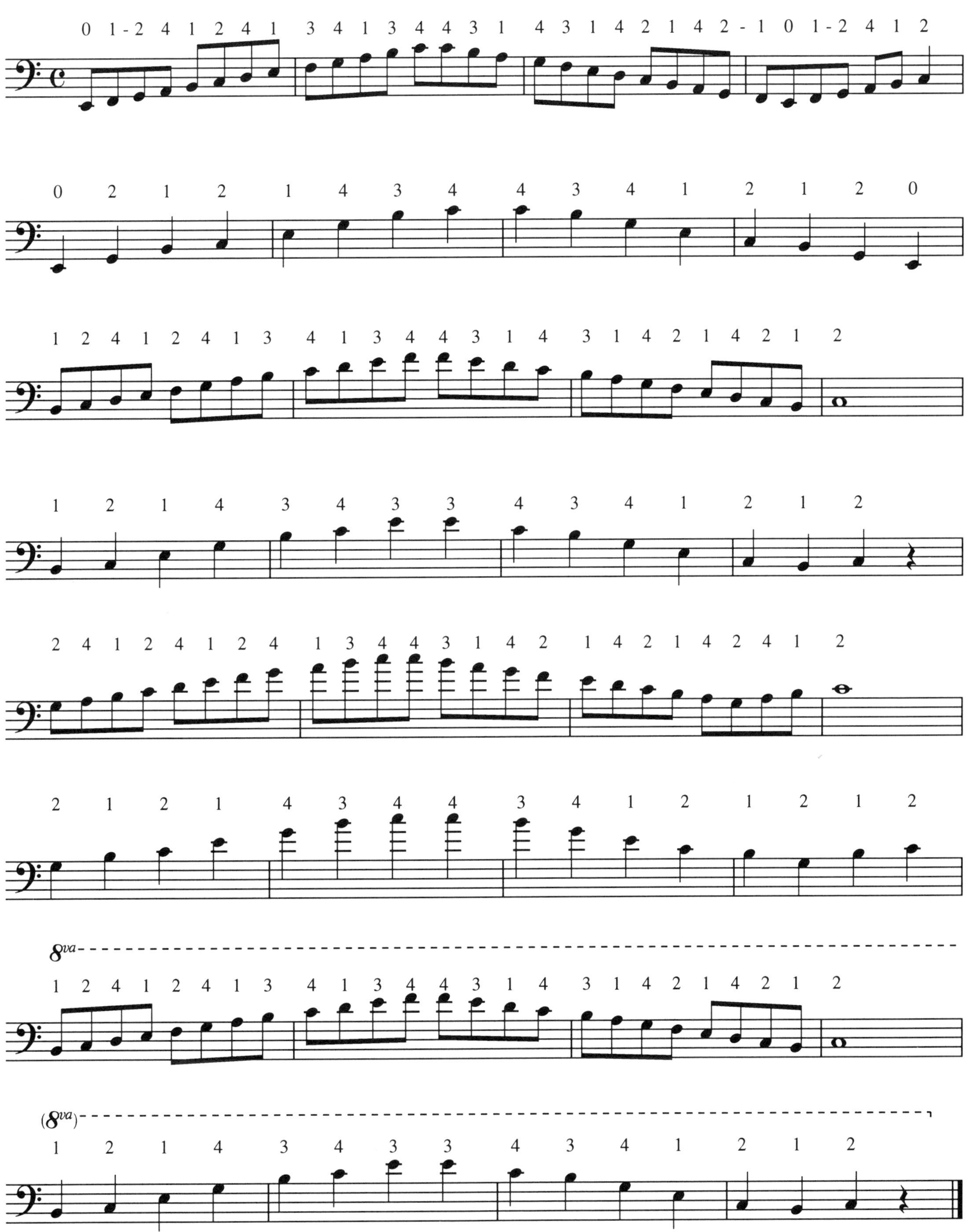

0 1 - 2 4 1 2 4 1 3 4 1 3 4 4 3 1 4 3 1 4 2 1 4 2 - 1 0 1 - 2 4 1 2
0 2 1 2 1 4 3 4 4 3 4 1 2 1 2 0
1 2 4 1 2 4 1 3 4 1 3 4 4 3 1 4 3 1 4 2 1 4 2 1 2
1 2 1 4 3 4 3 3 4 3 4 1 2 1 2
2 4 1 2 4 1 2 4 1 3 4 4 3 1 4 2 1 4 2 1 4 2 4 1 2
2 1 2 1 4 3 4 4 3 4 1 2 1 2 1 2
8va
1 2 4 1 2 4 1 3 4 1 3 4 4 3 1 4 3 1 4 2 1 4 2 1 2
(8va)
1 2 1 4 3 4 3 3 4 3 4 1 2 1 2

F Major

The first major scale and arpeggio is sort of different from what you saw in C Major. This is actually considered half position because you're not using a full position in that part of the fingerboard. This is okay though because you can take full advantage of those open strings. Be sure to follow my suggested fingerings too. The first and third patterns start you off on the seventh of the scale, E. The second and fourth patterns start you off on the fifth of the scale, C. Remember, key of F Major has one flat, B♭.

①

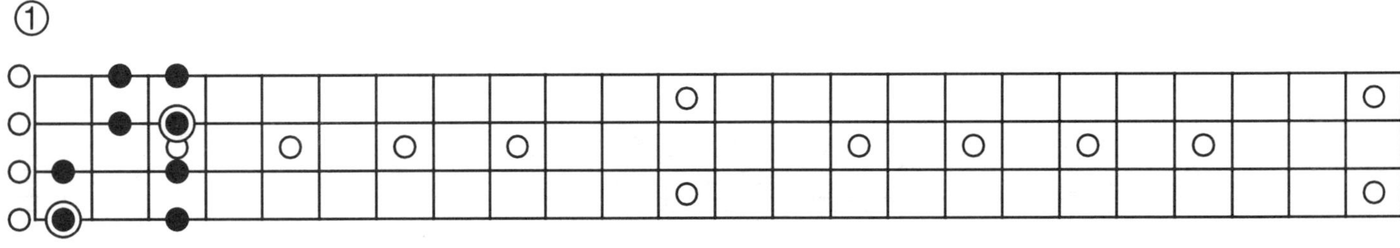

②

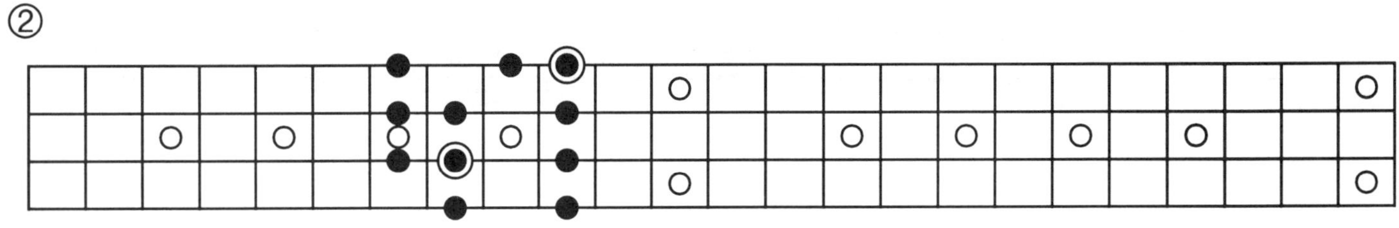

③

④

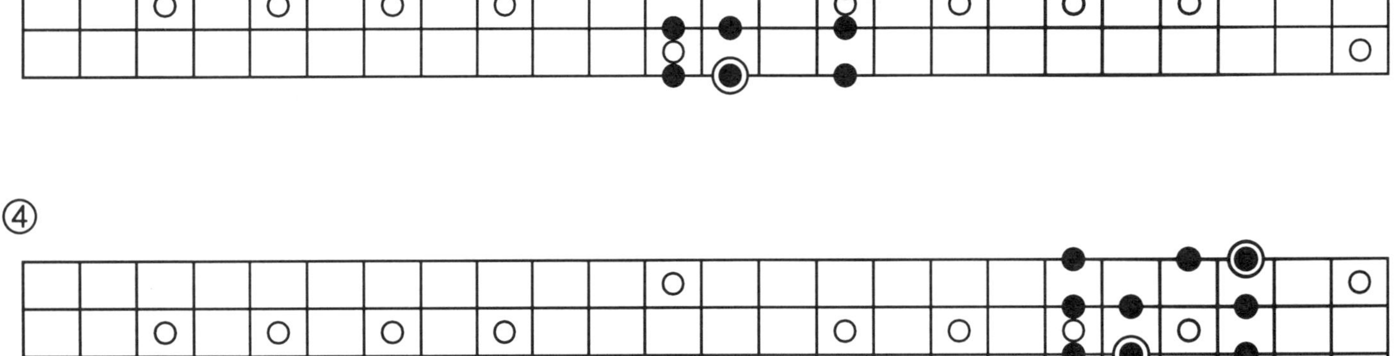

F Major

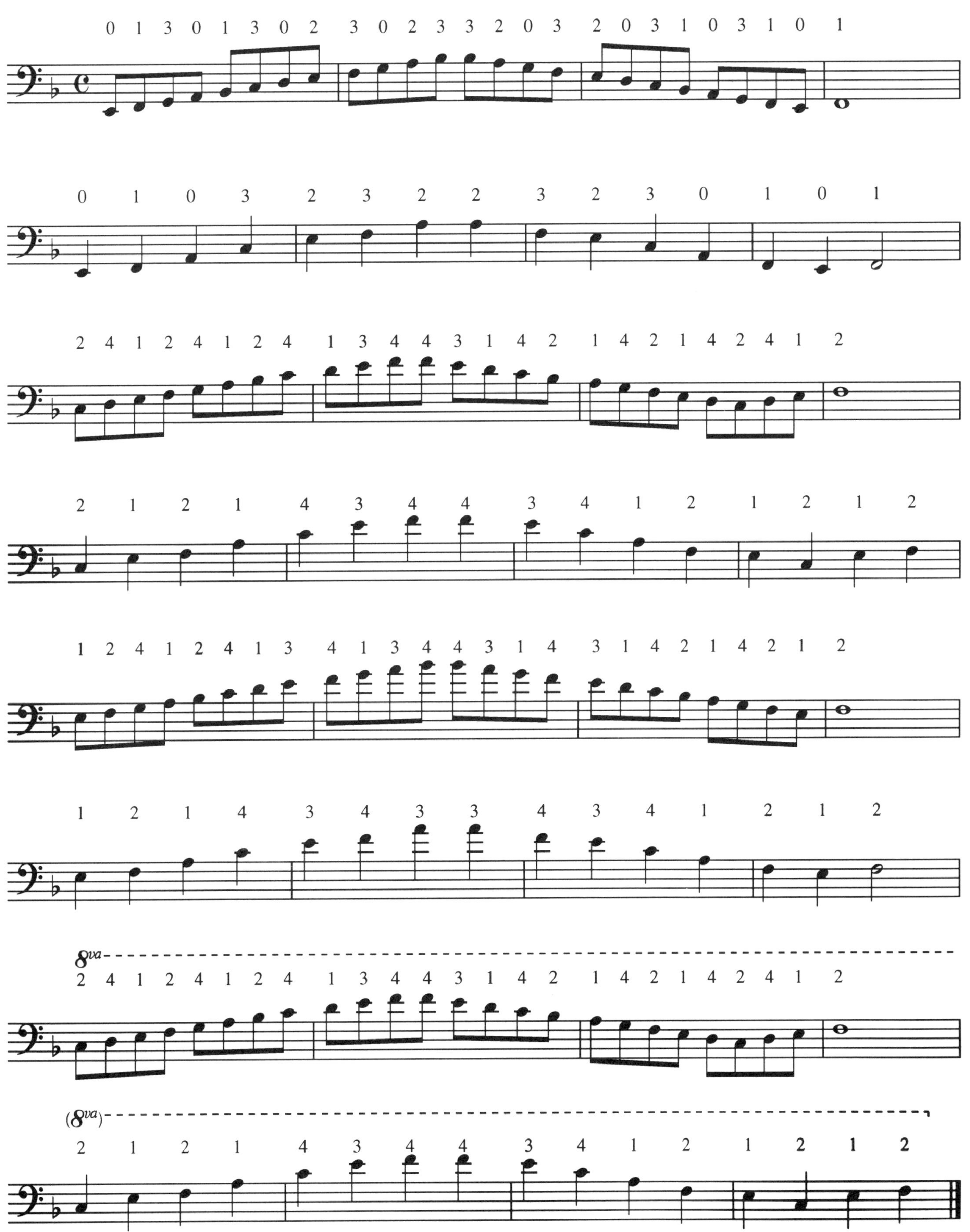

B♭ Major

Same thing that happened in F Major now happens in B♭ Major, the half position. Again, be sure to follow my fingerings as well as take advantage of those open strings too. The first and third patterns start you off on the fifth of the scale, F. The second and fourth patterns start you off on the seventh of the scale, A. Remember B♭ now has two flats, B♭ and E♭.

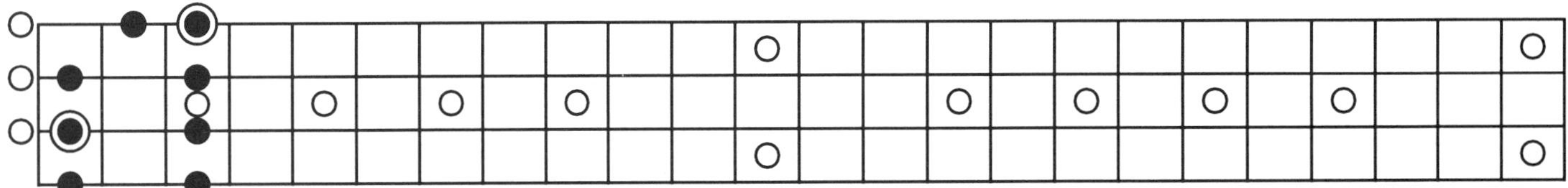

②

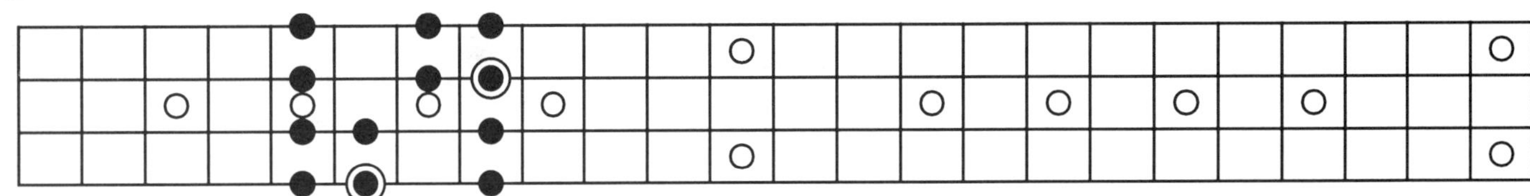

③

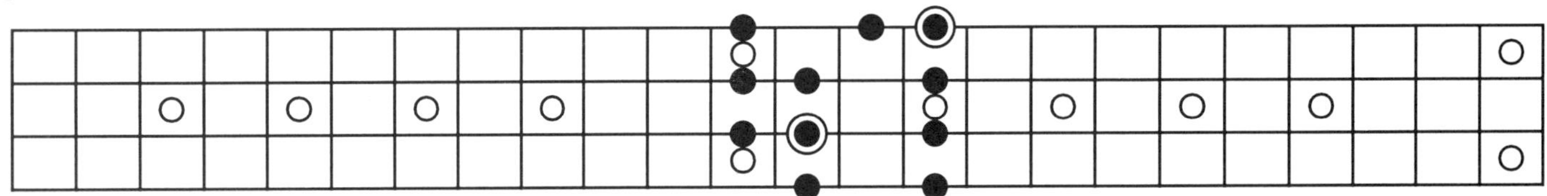

④

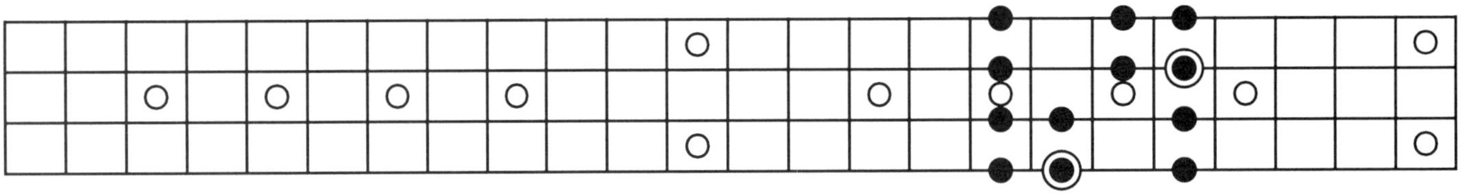

B♭ Major

E♭ Major

The E♭ Major scale and arpeggio takes us out of the half position and puts us in the normal patterns that we're used to seeing. You could try using the open strings for the first pattern. I recommend playing this first pattern with the closed strings though. This way you will also learn the third pattern as well. Take a look, the first and the third patterns start you off on the fifth of the scale, B♭, while the second and fourth patterns start you off on the seventh of the scale, D. Are you starting to see a formula develop yet?? E♭ has three flats, B♭, E♭, and A♭

①

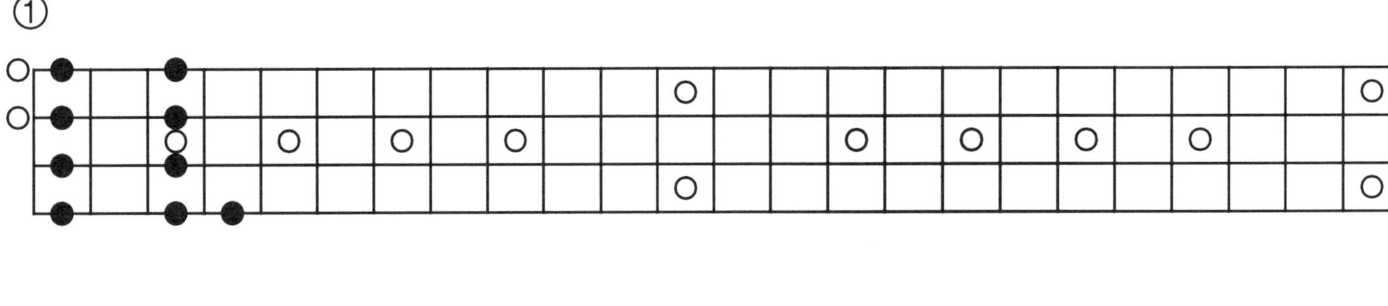

②

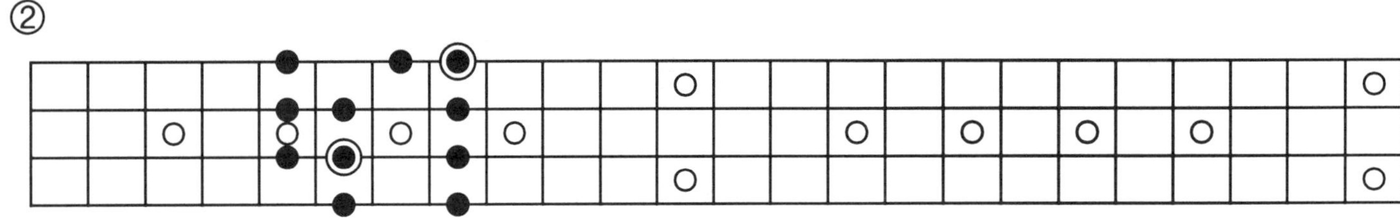

③

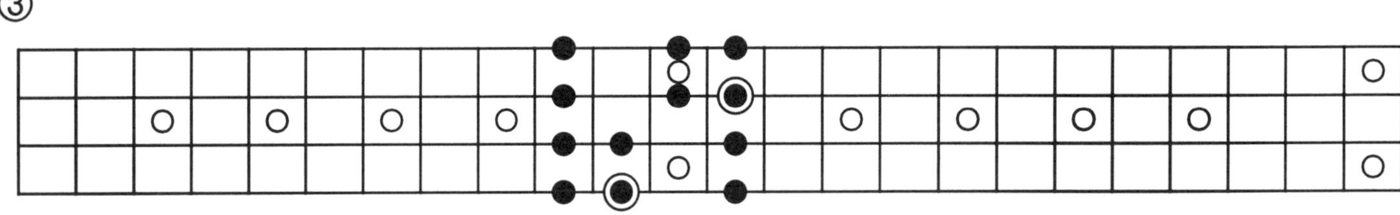

④

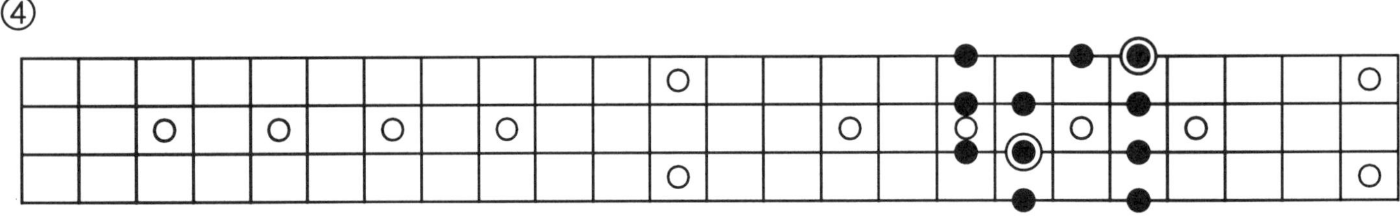

⑤

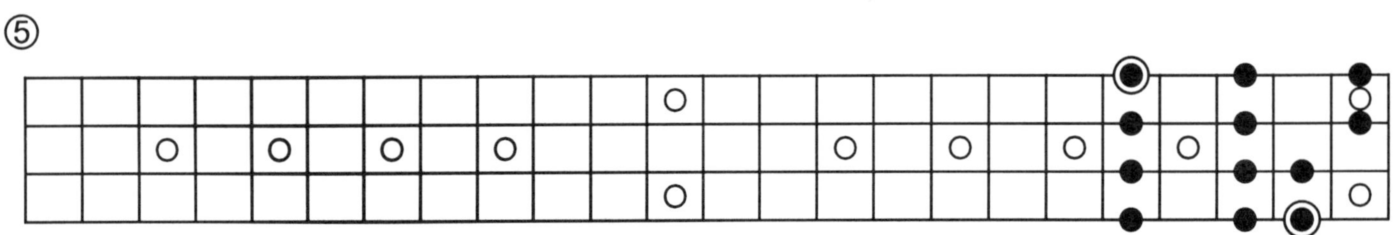

E♭ Major

1 3 4 1 3 0 1 3 0 1 3 3 1 0 3 1 0 3 1 4 3 1 3 4 1 3 0 1
3 1 0 1 0 3 3 0 1 0 1 3 1 0 1
8va
2 4 1 2 4 1 2 4 1 3 4 4 3 1 4 2 1 4 2 1 4 2 4 1 2
(8va)
2 1 2 1 4 3 4 4 3 4 1 2 1 2 1 2
1 2 4 1 2 4 1 3 4 1 3 4 4 3 1 4 3 1 4 2 1 4 2 1 2
1 2 1 4 3 4 3 3 4 3 4 1 2 1 2
1 3 4 1 3 4 1 3 - 4 1 3 - 4 4 - 3 1 4 - 3 1 4 3 1 4 3 1 3 4
8va
3 4 3 1 - 4 1 - 4 4 - 1 4 - 1 3 4 3 4

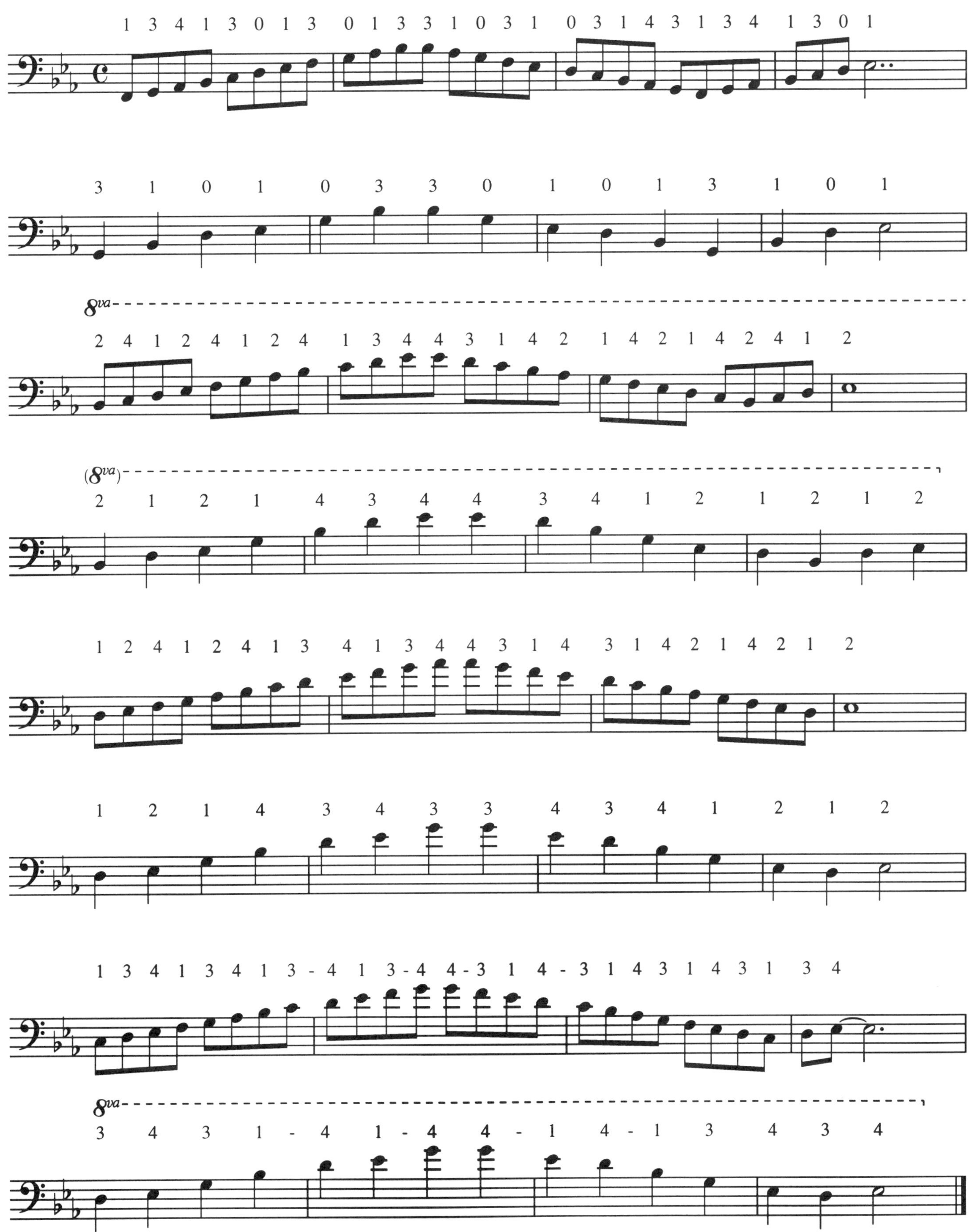

A♭ Major

A♭ Major is pretty straight ahead as well. This time the first and third patterns start out on the seventh of the scale while the second pattern starts out on the fifth. The tricky pattern here is the fourth pattern . This starts out on the third below the root of the scale. This pattern isn't a typical pattern but I put it in because you should get used to knowing the notes outside of these patterns as well. You also have one note outside of the four fret range as well, the G-24-G. Being that the frets are so close together at this part of the fingerboard, you should be able to stretch out a bit. Just be sure to follow my fingerings on the pattern. A♭ has four flats, B♭, E♭, A♭ and D♭.

①

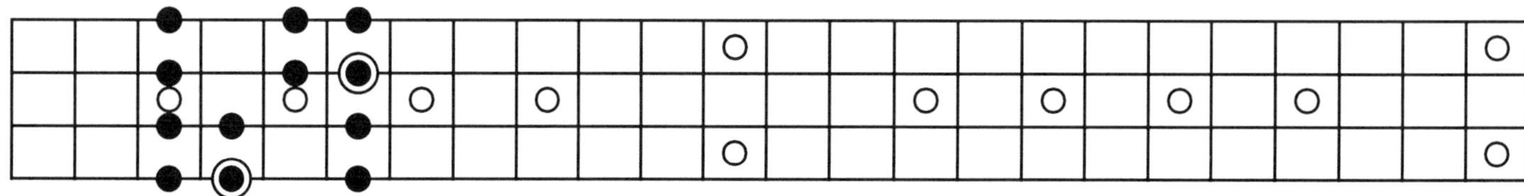

②

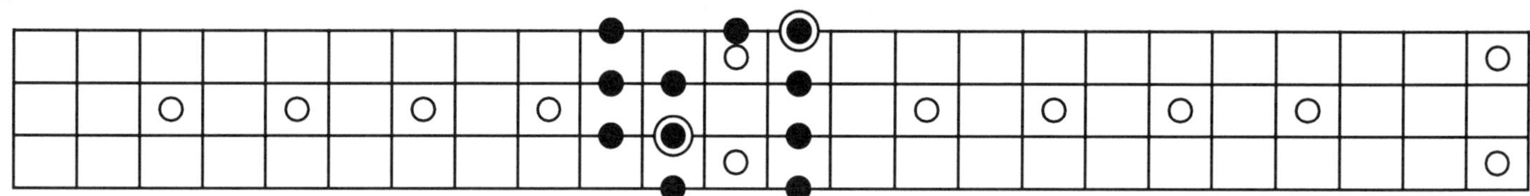

③

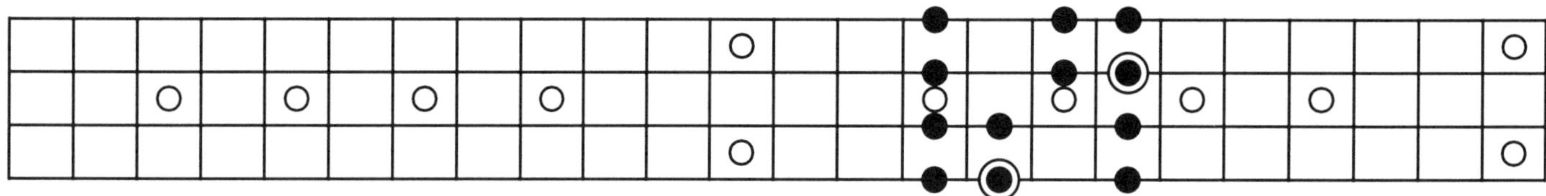

④

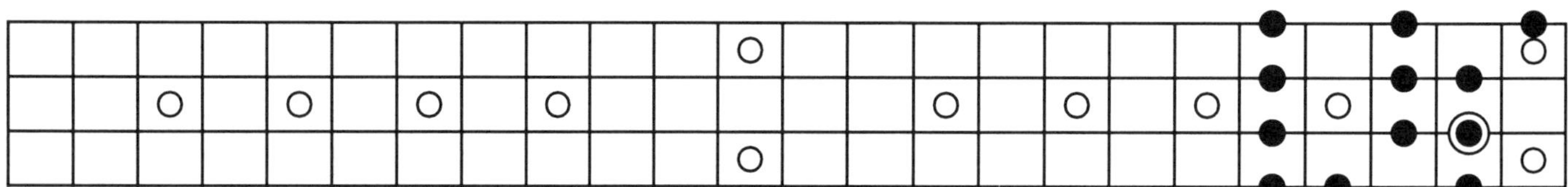

A♭ Major

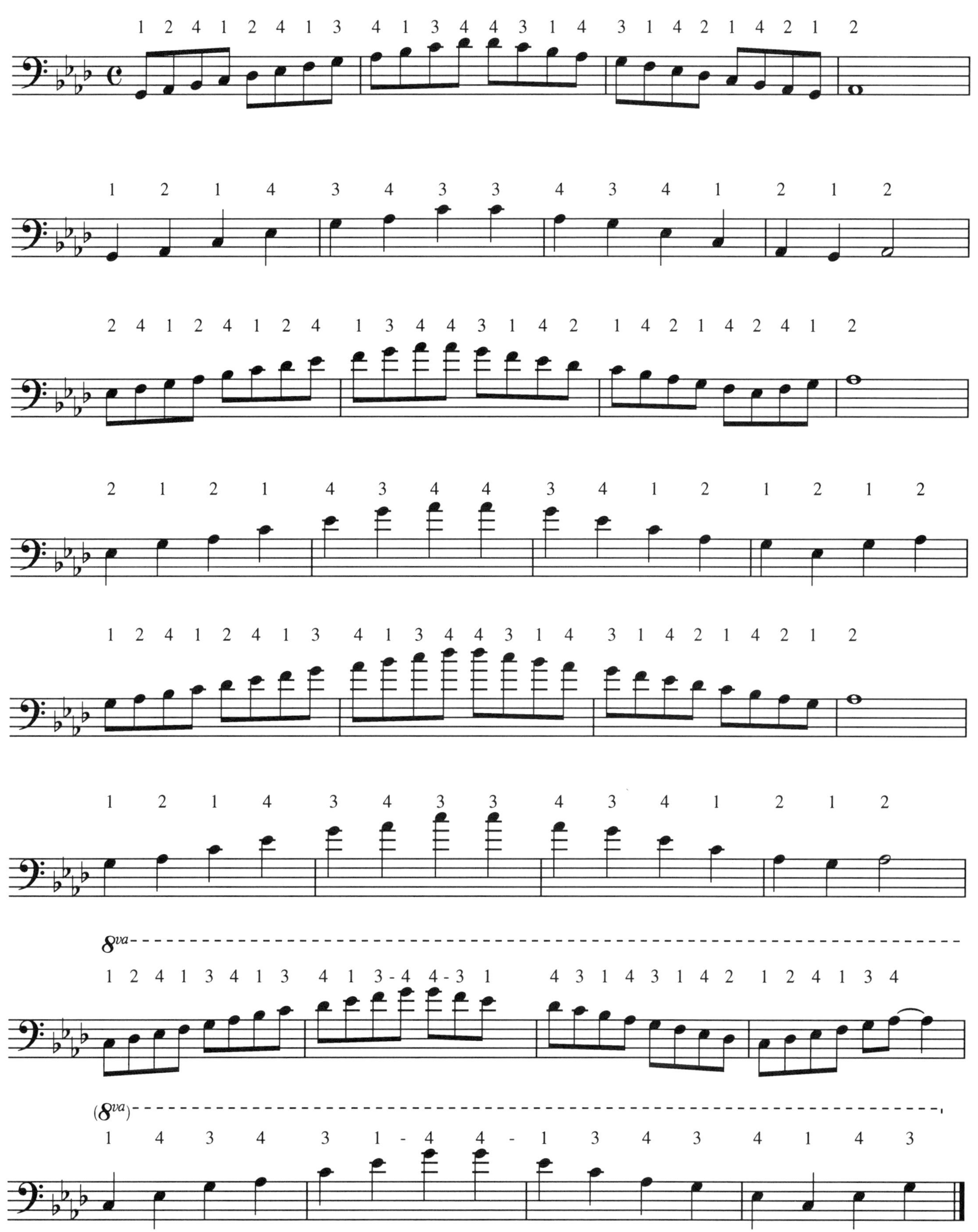

D♭ Major/C♯ Major

D♭ Major brings us back to some normal patterns. The first and third patterns start off on the fifth of the scale, A♭. And the second and the fourth patterns start you off on the seventh of the scale C. Remember to follow the fingerings in scale and arpeggio patterns. D♭ Major has five flats, B♭, E♭, A♭, D♭ and G♭.

The enharmonic of D♭ Major is C♯ Major. Although none of the fingering patterns have changed, the notation certainly has. Now instead of having five flats, you've got seven sharps. F♯, C♯, G♯, D♯, A♯, E♯ and B♯. Also the fifth of the scale has changed, instead of it being A♭, it's now G♯. The seventh also changed from C to B♯. Practice these scales and arpeggios in both enharmonics so you will get familiar with their content.

①

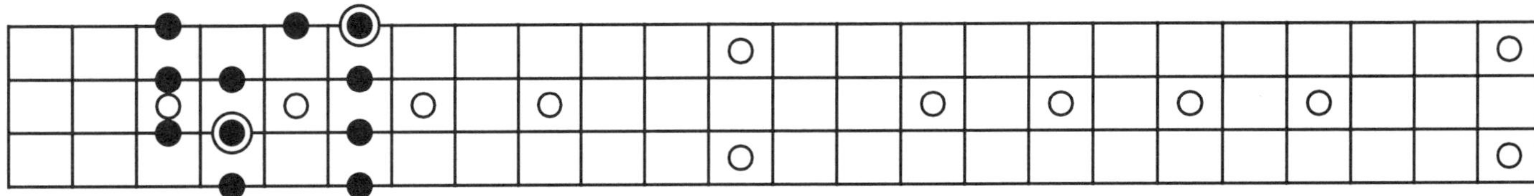

②

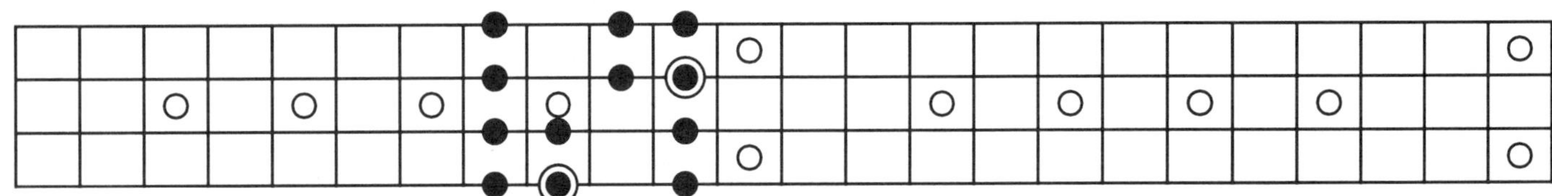

③

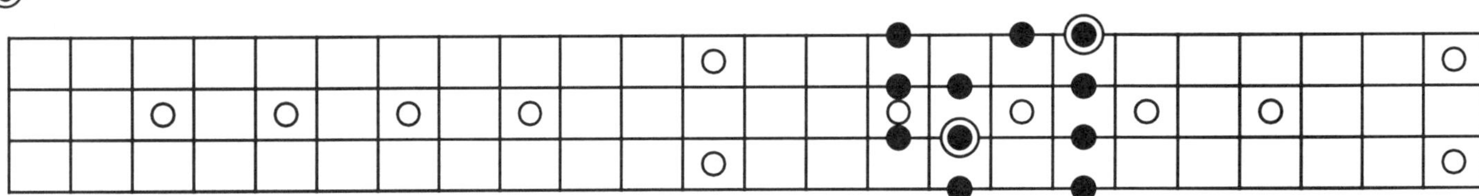

④

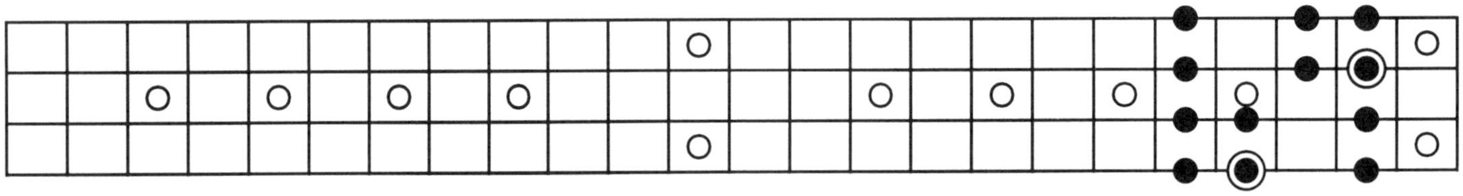

D♭ Major

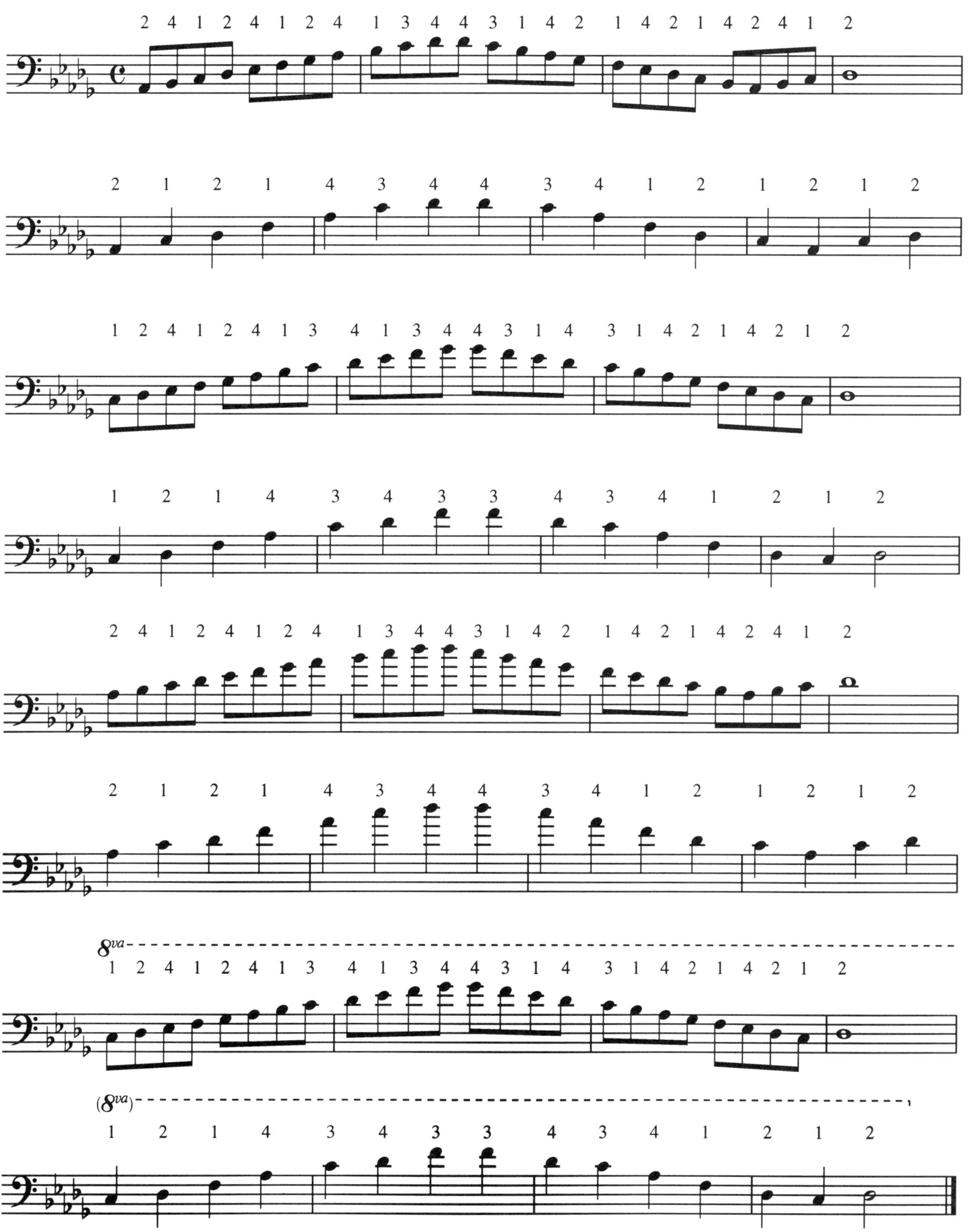

C♯ Major

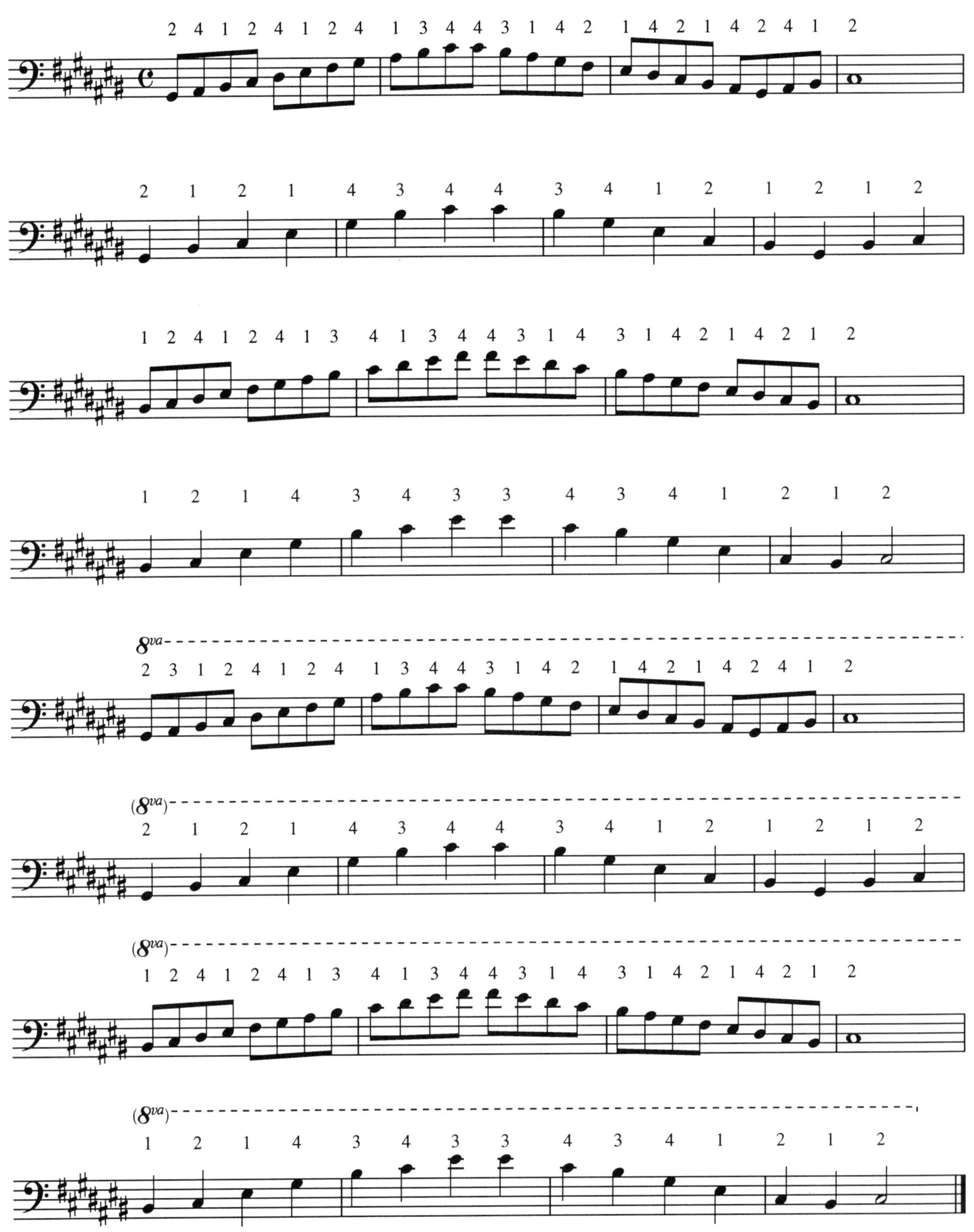

G♭/F♯ Major

Next up is G♭ as well as F♯ Major. Let's start with G♭ first. All of the patterns you should be familiar with by now and be able to play them in your sleep. The first and third patterns start you off on the seventh of the scale, F. The second and the fourth patterns start you off on the fifth of the scale, D♭. G♭ has six flats, B♭, E♭, A♭, D♭, G♭ and C♭.

F♯ again contains the same fingering patterns but the notation has changed. The first and third patterns are now starting on E♯, and the second and fourth patterns are starting on C♯. F♯ contains six sharps, F♯, C♯, G♯, D♯, A♯ and E♯.

①

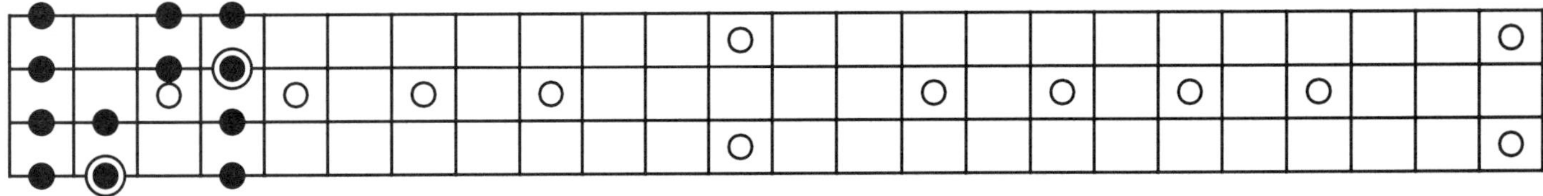

②

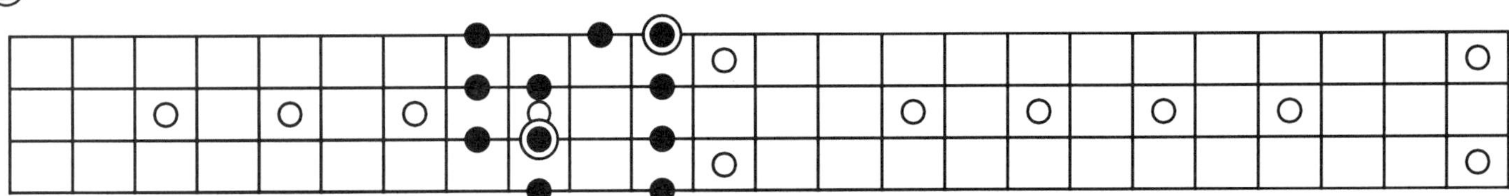

③

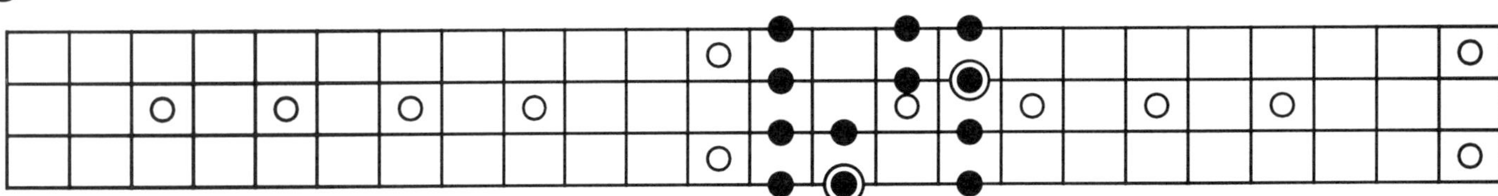

④

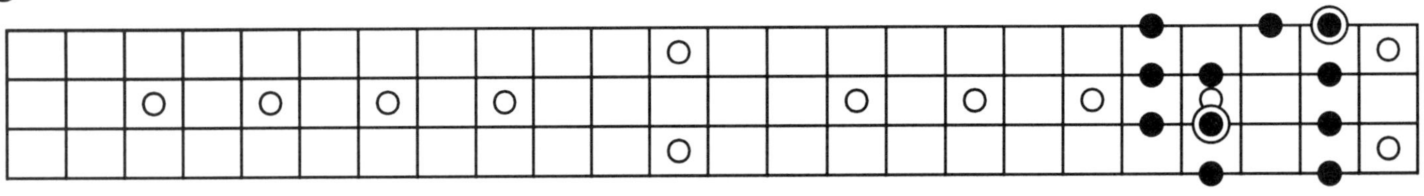

G♭ Major

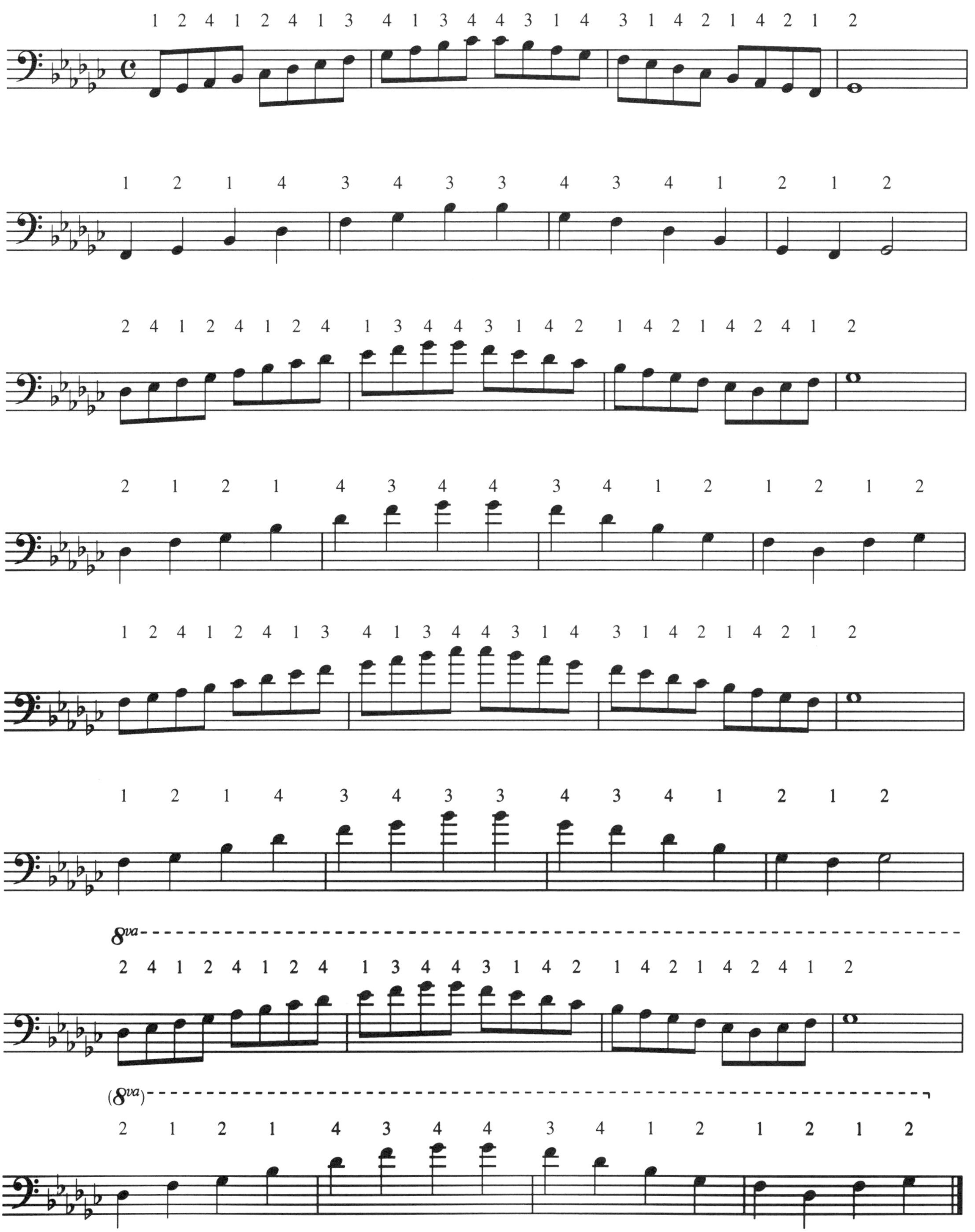

F♯ Major

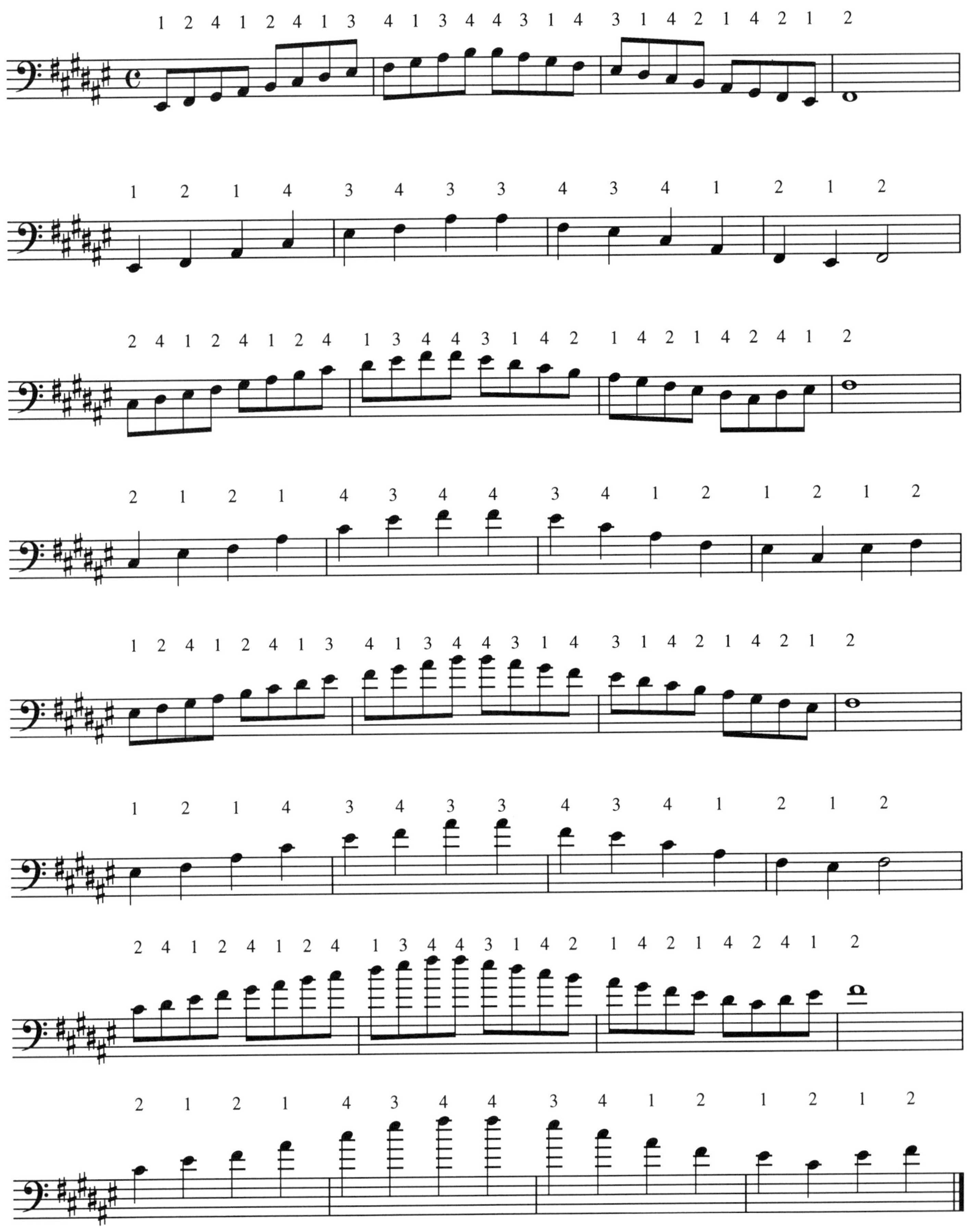

C♭/B Major

This will be the last of the enharmonic keys for now. Again we'll start with the flat key first, C♭. You'll notice that in C♭, ALL of the notes are flat, or lowered 1/2 step. The patterns still remain the same though. In the first pattern, take advantage of the open E string, however in the key of C♭, it's actually an F♭. So now we can say that the first pattern starts off on the fourth of the scale, F♭. The remaining three patterns are straight ahead. The second and fourth patterns starts you off on the seventh of the scale, B♭. The third pattern starts you off on the fifth of the scale, G♭. C♭ Major has seven flats, B♭, E♭, A♭, D♭, G♭, C♭ and F♭.

The enharmonic of C♭ is B. Again, same patterns, just different notation and actually easier because B Major has only five sharps as opposed to C♭ Major's seven flats. Now we can call that fourth open string E, which still starts us off on the fourth of the scale. The second and fourth patterns start you off on the seventh of the scale, A♯. The third pattern starts you off on the fifth of the scale as well, F♯. B Major has five sharps, F♯, C♯, G♯, D♯ and A♯. Remember to follow my fingerings and say the notes as you play them.

①

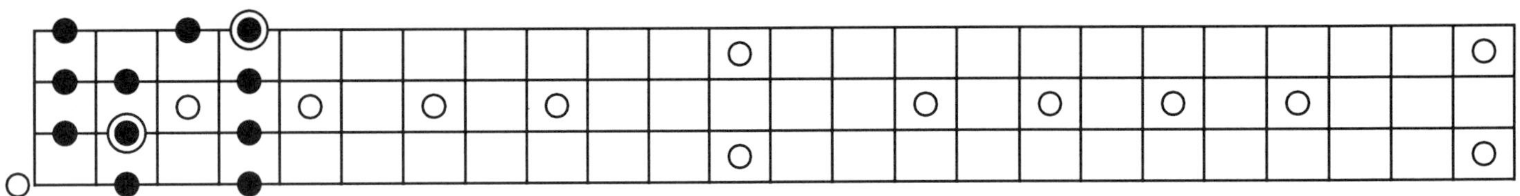

②

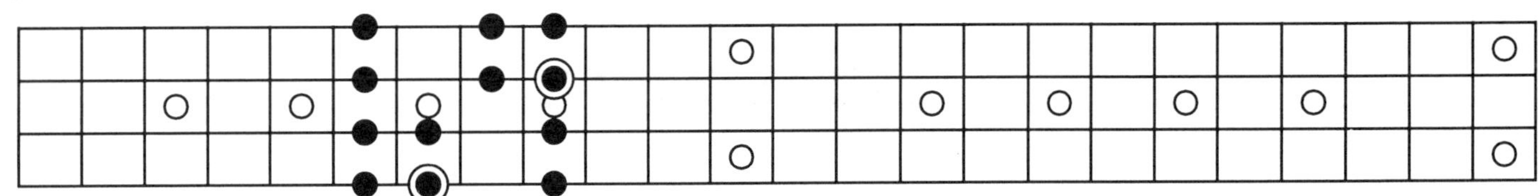

③

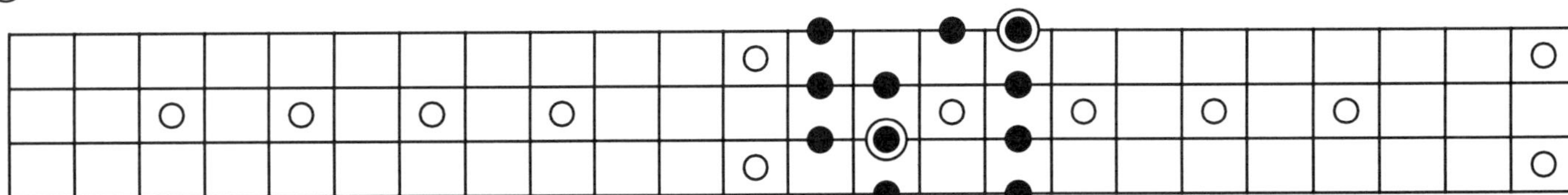

④

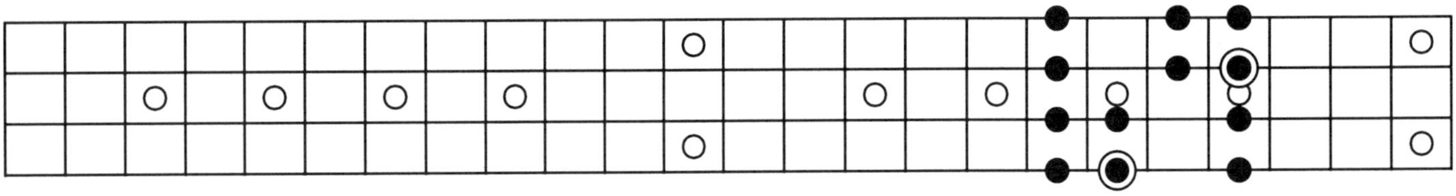

C♭ Major

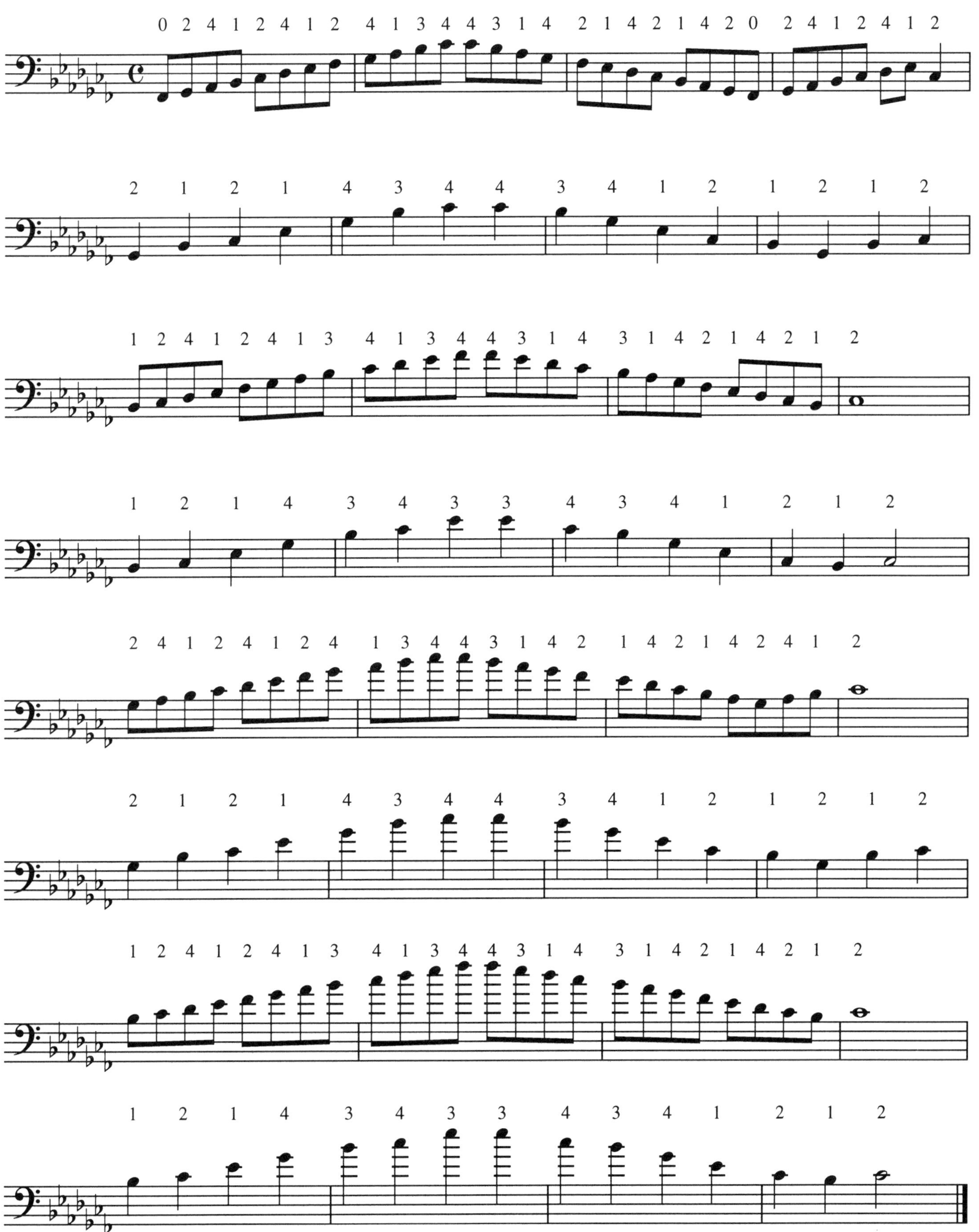

B Major

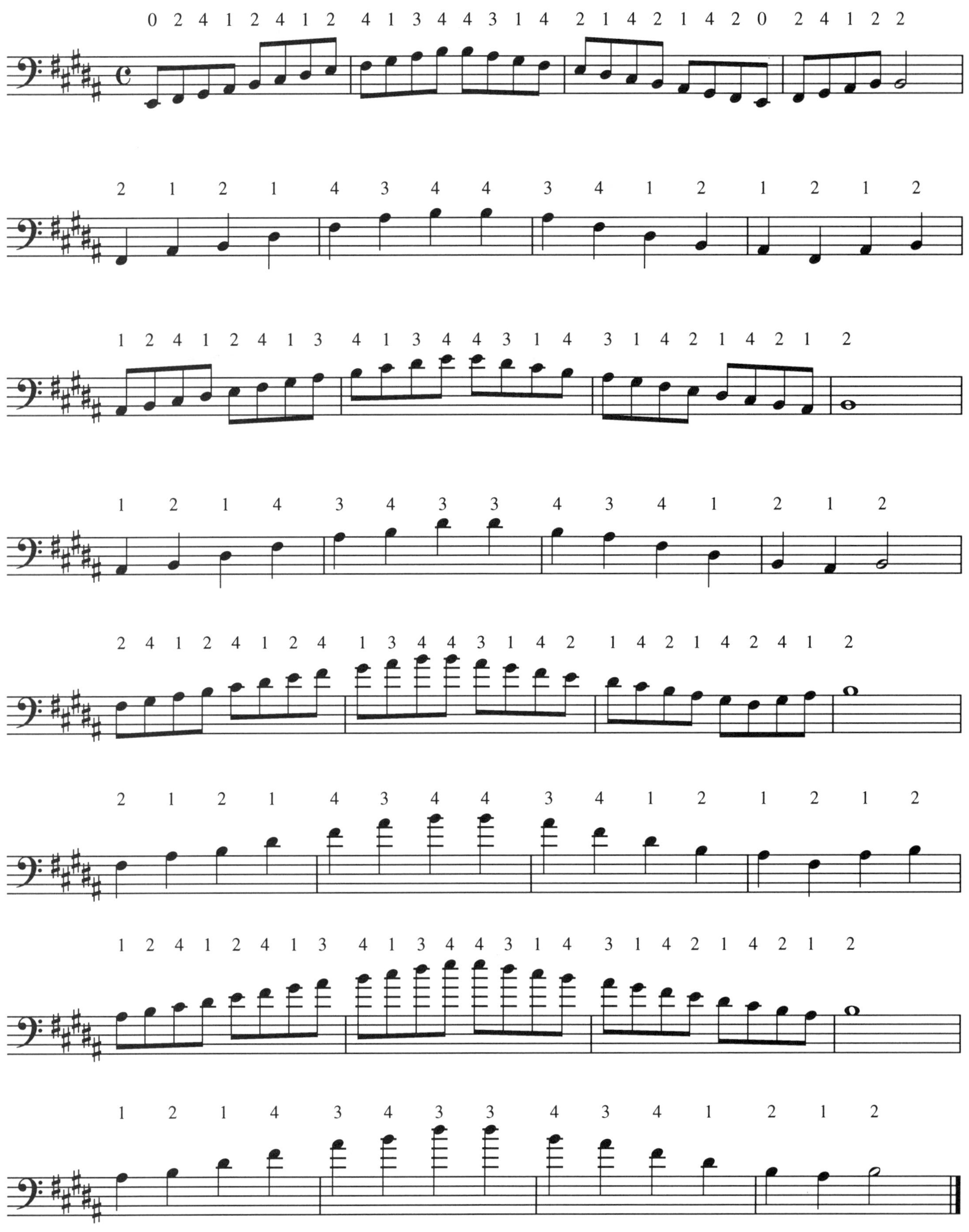

E Major

Next on the circle we've got E Major. Be sure to take advantage of the two open strings in the first pattern. You can still use the one finger per fret method if you stick to using the open strings in this one. Just be sure to follow my fingerings. This pattern will start you off on the root of the scale, E. The second and fourth patterns are straight ahead as well, they get you started on the fifth of the scale, B. The third pattern is familiar too, this gets you started on the seventh of the scale, D♯. You've probably noticed that there is a fifth pattern too. If you have a bass with only twenty or twenty-one frets don't worry about this pattern. If you've got a bass with twenty-four frets, let's take a look. This pattern will start you off on the sixth of the scale, C♯, but you've got to use some creative fingerings to be able to play the whole pattern. If you have a hard time getting to that C♯ on the E string, try bringing your thumb around to the front of the fingerboard. If that doesn't work, try to get just the notes on the D and G string. Be sure to follow my fingerings on this one. You will have to shift out of position to get to that D♯ on the G string but that's okay. E Major has four sharps, F♯, C♯, G♯ and D♯.

①

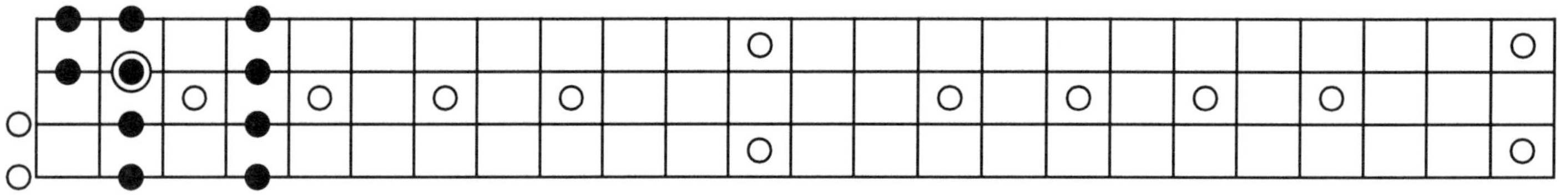

②

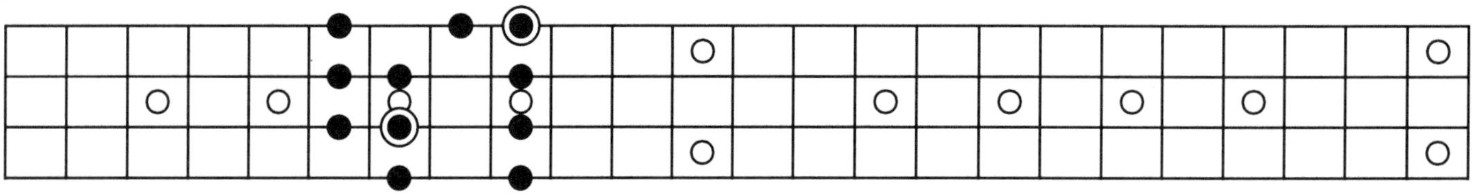

③

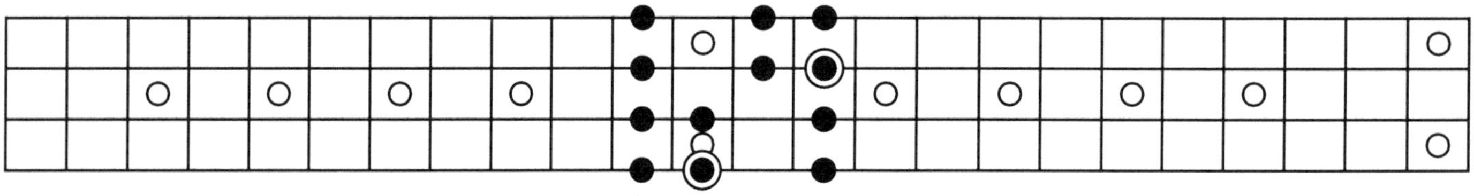

④

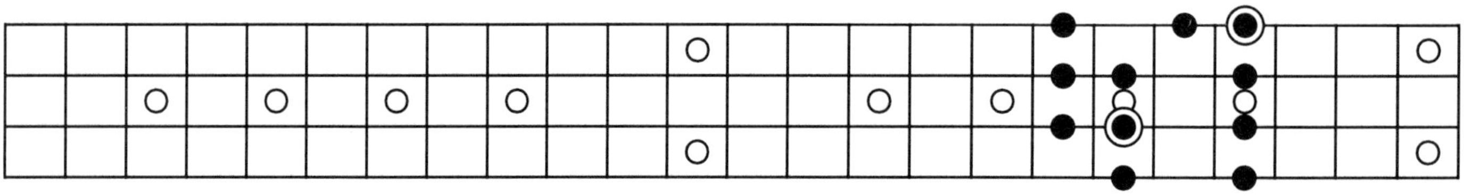

⑤

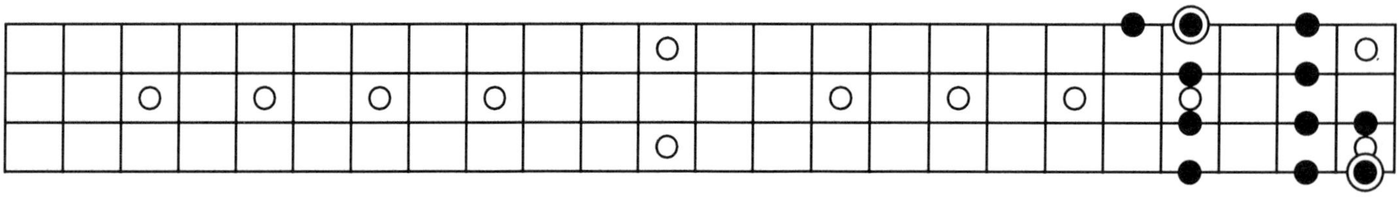

E Major

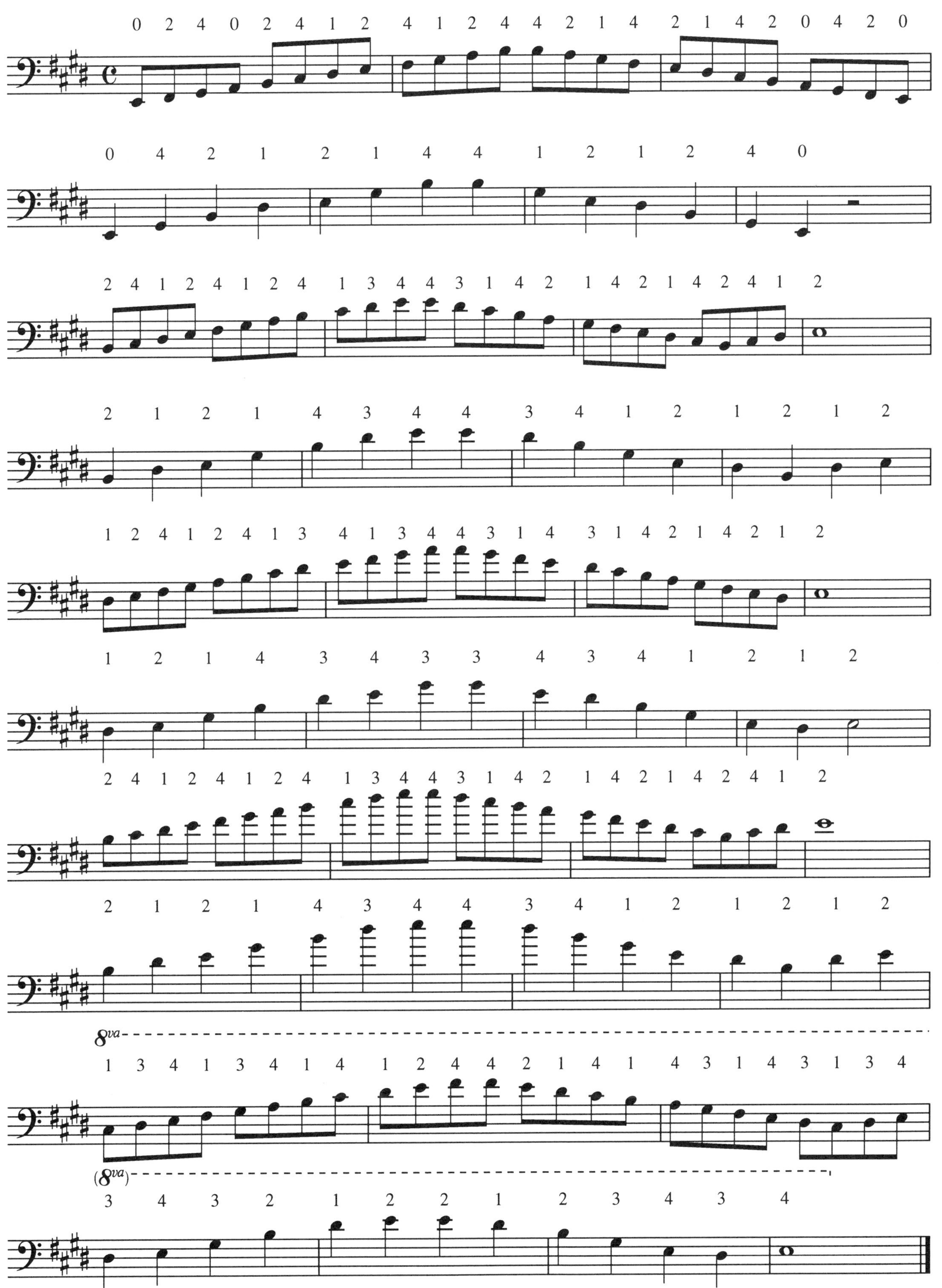

A Major

Notice that as we get further into the sharp keys, the number of sharps in each key get lower and lower. A Major has only three sharps, F♯, C♯ and G♯. The patterns are pretty standard too except for the fourth pattern. The fourth pattern starts you off on the third of the scale, C♯. This is similar to the pattern you saw in E Major. Like I had said before, this will only work with a bass with a twenty-four fret neck. If you have a hard time reaching that C♯, try bringing your thumb around to the front of the fingerboard. If that doesn't work, try to get just the notes on the D and G string.

①

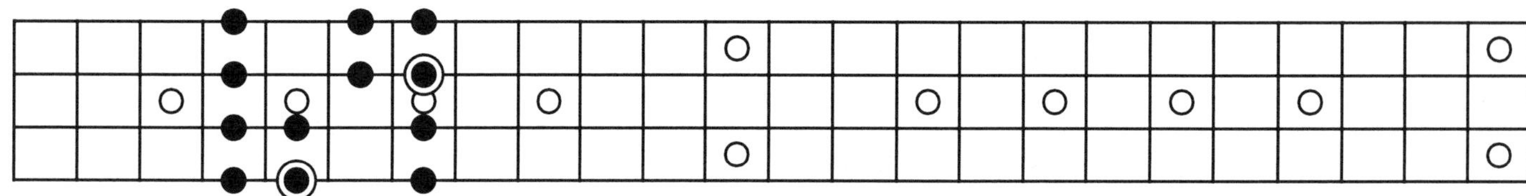

②

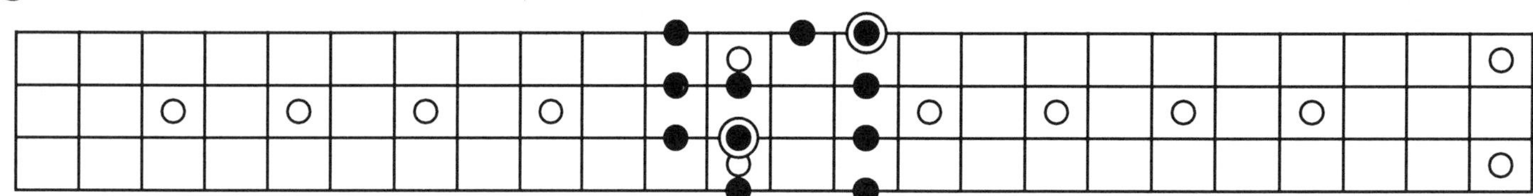

③

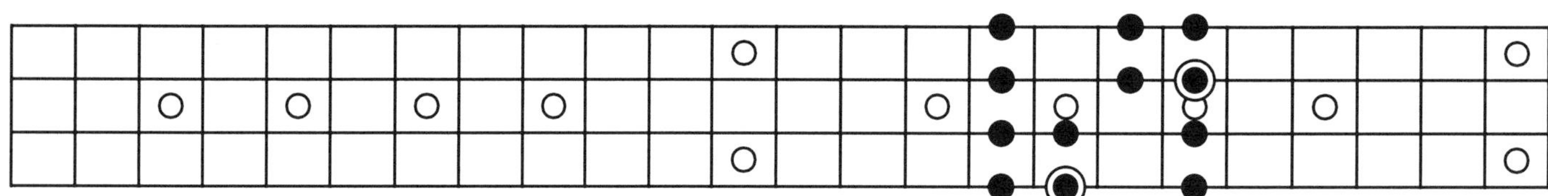

④

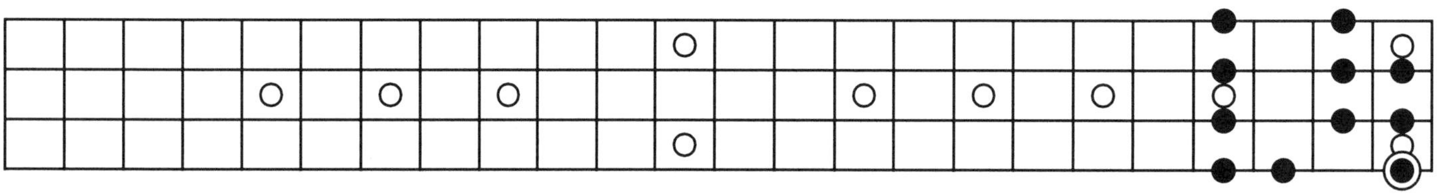

A Major

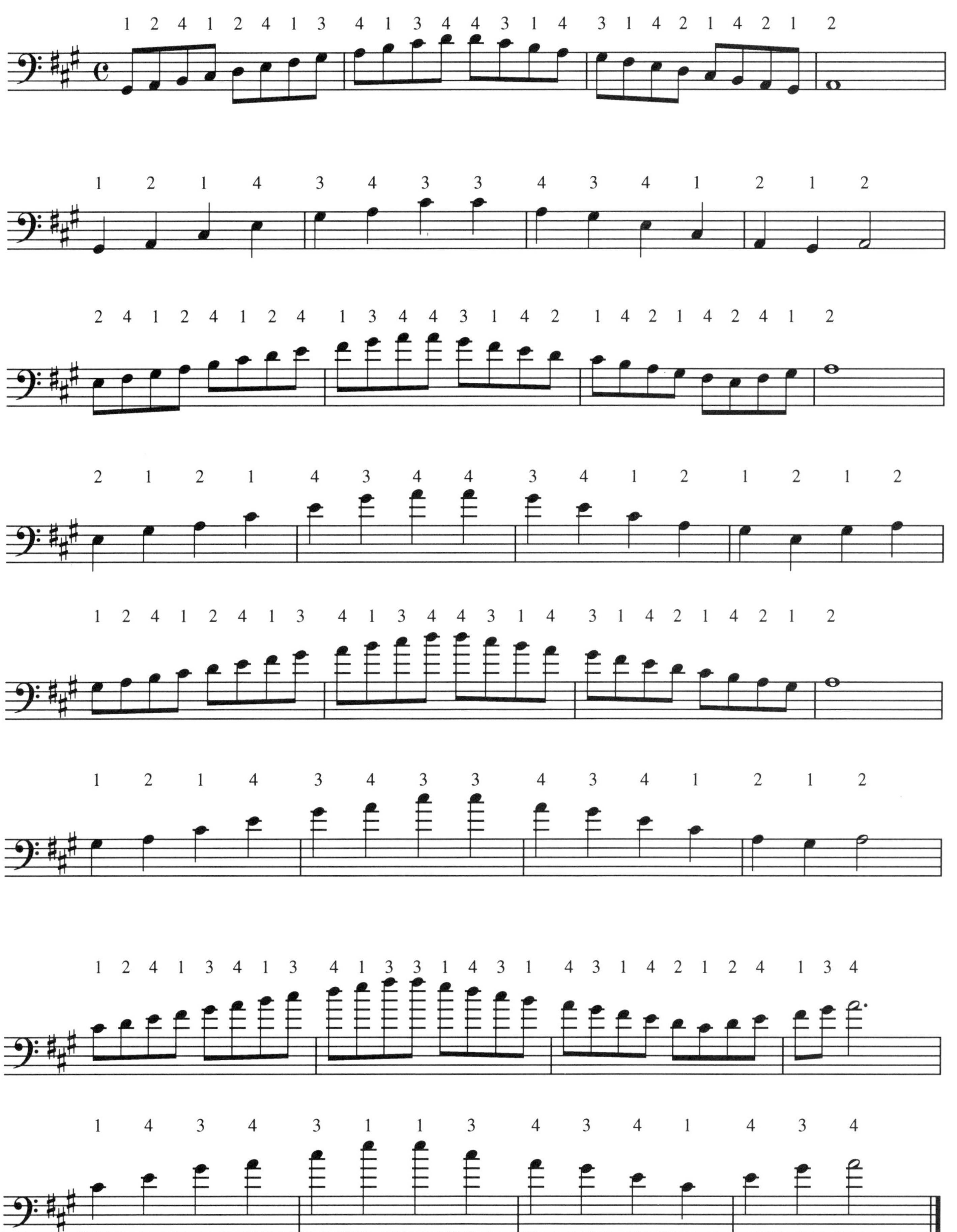

D Major

The second to last key is D major. D Major has only two sharps, F♯ and C♯. The patterns are very familiar as well. You should have no problems with this one. The first and third patterns start off on the fifth of the scale, A. And the second and the fourth patterns start off on the seventh of the scale, C♯. Remember, follow my fingerings and say the notes as you play them

①

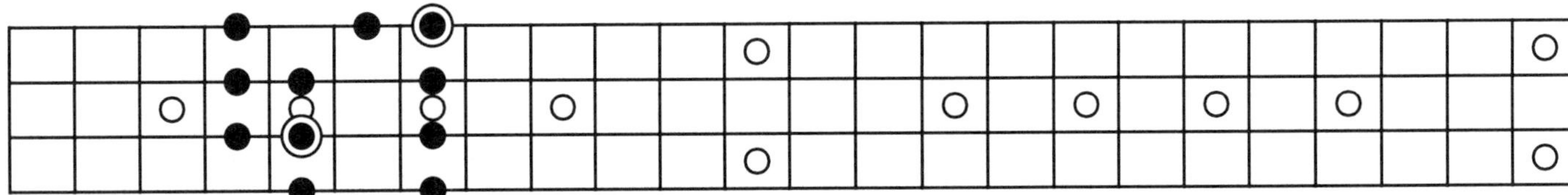

②

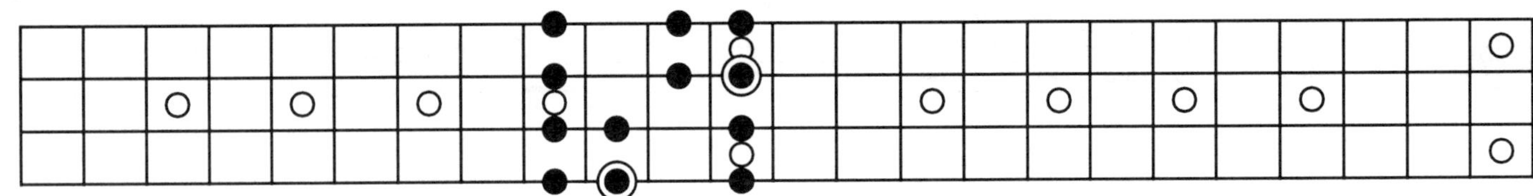

③

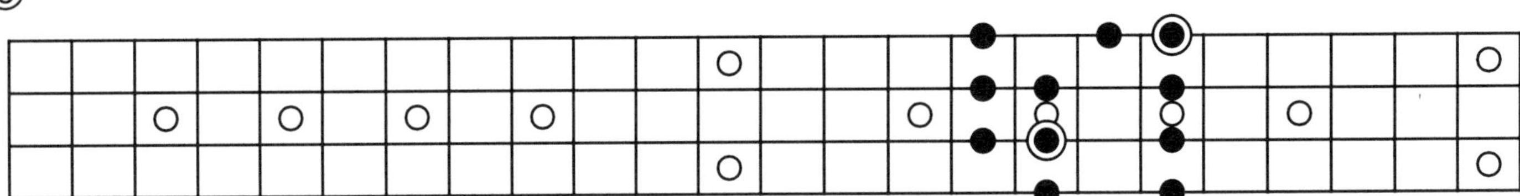

④

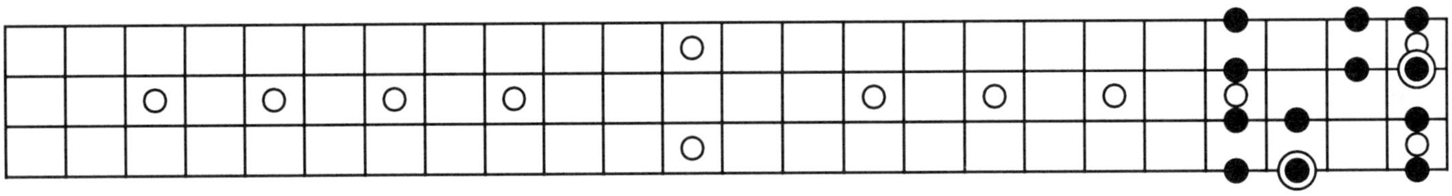

D Major

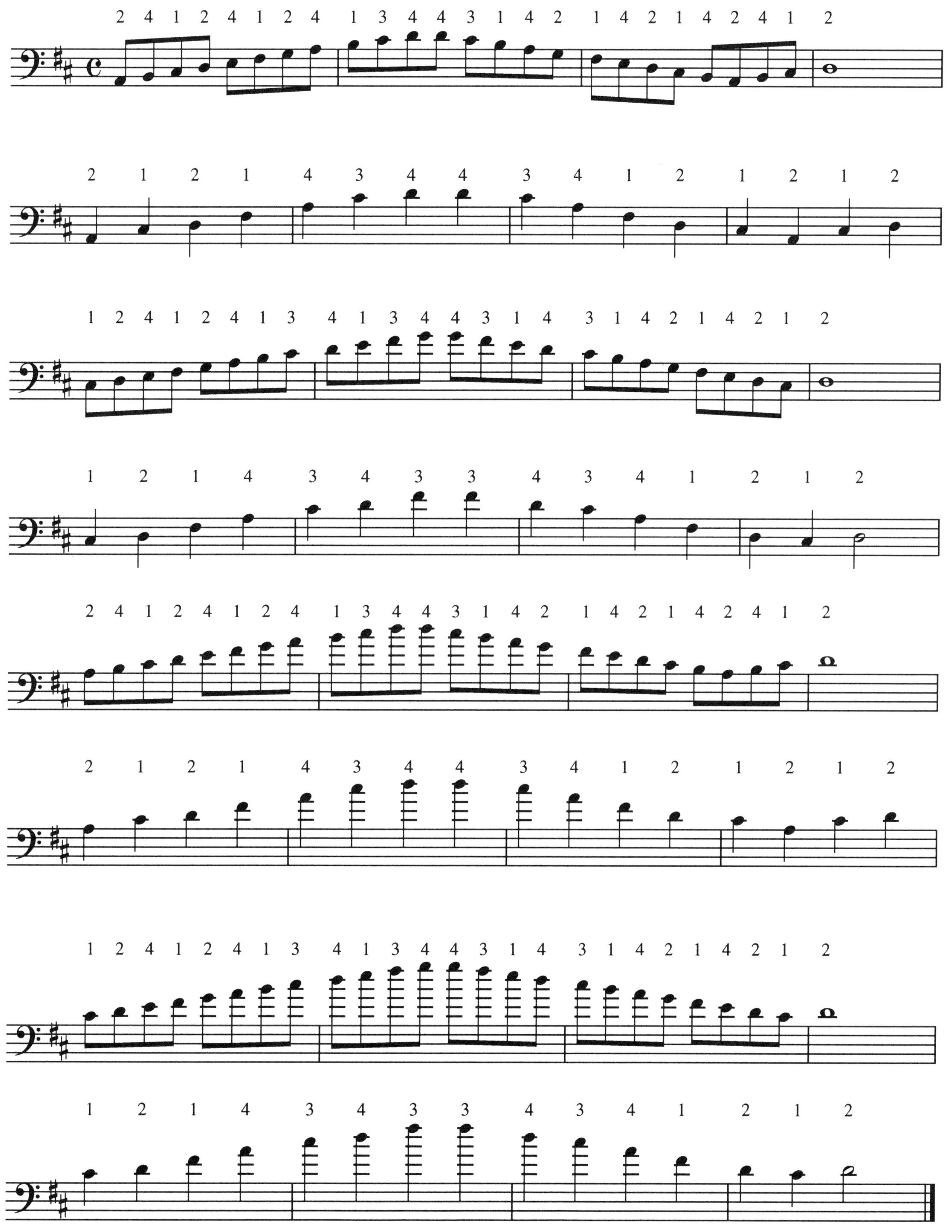

G Major

Last but not least we have G Major, the easiest sharp key to remember. One sharp, F♯. All of the patterns are the same as what you have learned. The first and third patterns start off on the seventh of the scale, F♯. The second and fourth pattern start off on the fifth of the scale, D. Follow my fingerings and say the notes as you play them!!! Have Fun!!!!

①

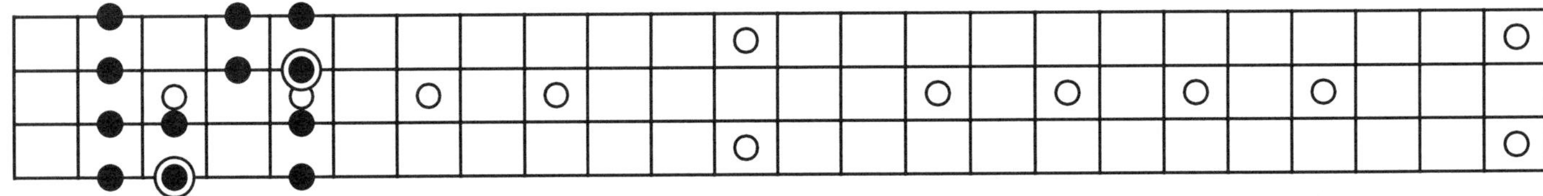

②

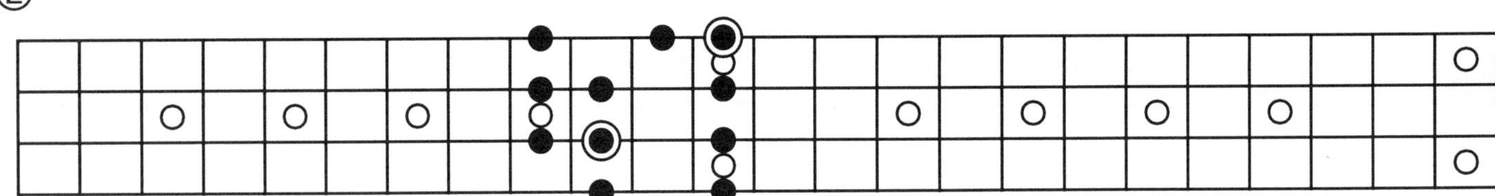

③

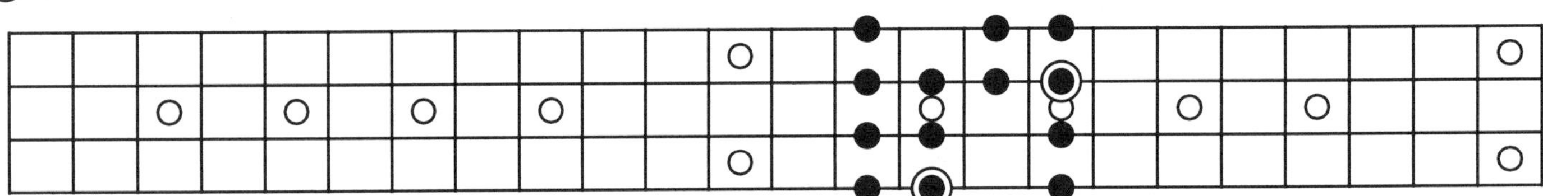

④

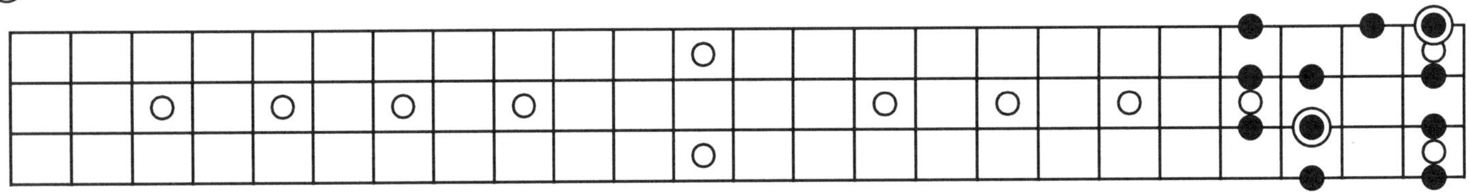

G Major

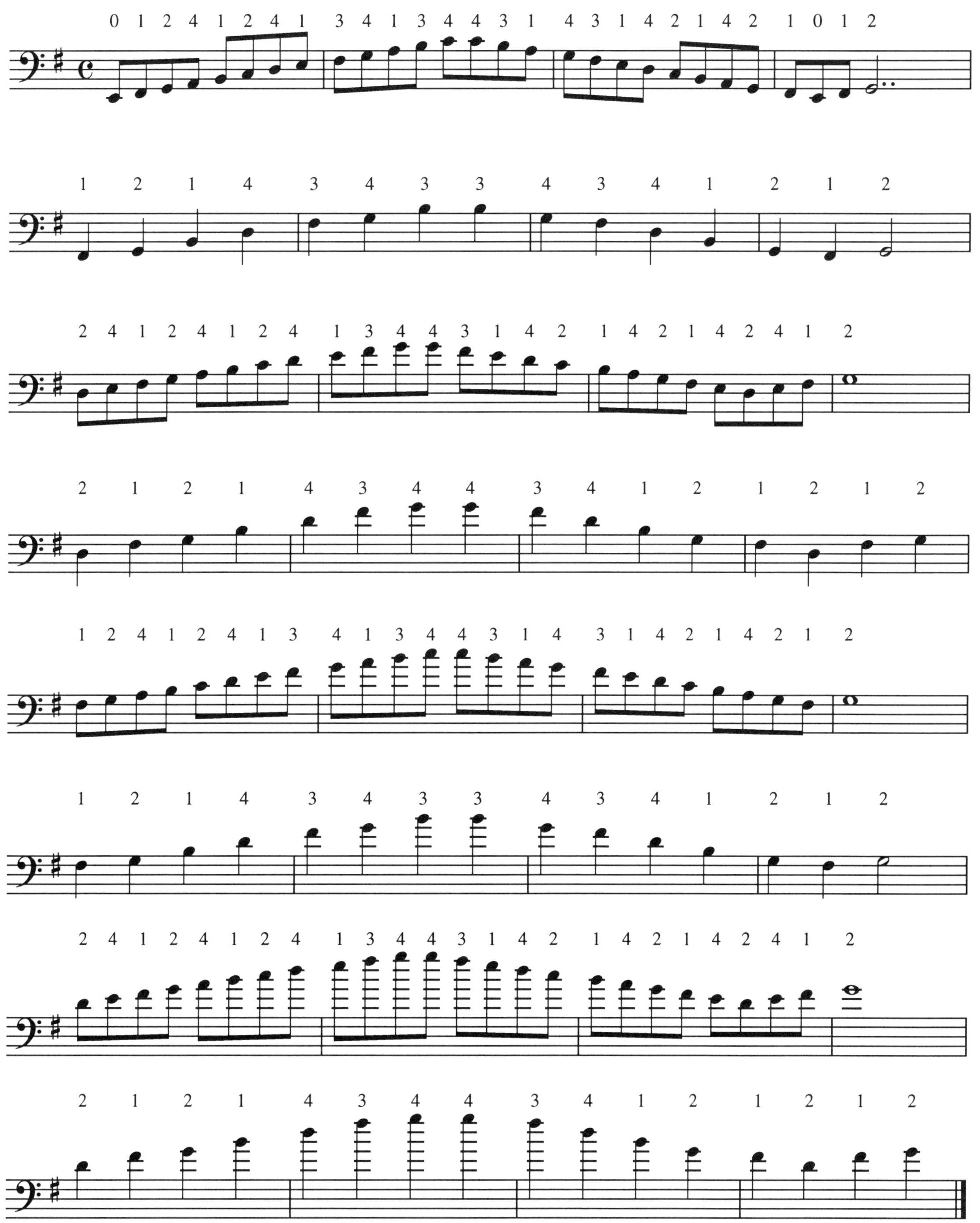

0 1 2 4 1 2 4 1 3 4 1 3 4 4 3 1 4 3 1 4 2 1 4 2 1 0 1 2
1 2 1 4 3 4 3 3 4 3 4 1 2 1 2
2 4 1 2 4 1 2 4 1 3 4 4 3 1 4 2 1 4 2 1 4 2 4 1 2
2 1 2 1 4 3 4 4 3 4 1 2 1 2 1 2
1 2 4 1 2 4 1 3 4 1 3 4 4 3 1 4 3 1 4 2 1 4 2 1 2
1 2 1 4 3 4 3 3 4 3 4 1 2 1 2
2 4 1 2 4 1 2 4 1 3 4 4 3 1 4 2 1 4 2 1 4 2 4 1 2
2 1 2 1 4 3 4 4 3 4 1 2 1 2 1 2

Single String Studies

Okay, now that you've got the major scales and arpeggios down in one octave and in full positions up the neck, the next step is to learn them up and down each individual string.

What we will do in this chapter is learn all twelve major scales and arpeggios up and down each individual string. This is the best way to compliment what you have learned so far and should be one of the final steps in connecting all of the positions that you have learned. After all, you don't want to be restricted to only being able to play any major scale in just one position or one octave for that matter. The object is to be able to connect all of the major scales up and down the neck. Try to think of your neck as one entire position for each key.

For each key you will see two pages, one that has the fingering diagram for each string starting with the G string at the top of the page and the E string on the bottom. Just as if you were laying your bass on your lap. On the other page the actual notation for each major scale and the notation for each major 7 arpeggio below each scale. Each string will show you all of the available notes in the respective scale. Remember, the name of the scale doesn't necessarily designate the note that you will start on for each string. For instance, playing a C major scale up and down the G string, you would start the scale on the open G which is the fifth of the C major scale. This is where your knowledge of the past two chapters comes into play. You need to know the actual notes in a C major scale as well as all of the other scales too. The open circle at the beginning of the string indicates an open string to be played. You will also notice the 8va above some of the notation. Because of the range of the electric bass, I didn't want to have to write more than four ledger lines above the staff. The 8va tells you to play the written notes up one octave!

You will also see the fingerings for each major scale and the fingerings for each major 7 arpeggio below each staff. **Make sure to follow the fingerings I've given you.** I've found these to be the most logical without too many shifts. Once you get comfortable with the single string exercises, go ahead and experiment with your own fingerings. **The dashes in between some of the sequences of numbers indicates a shift.**

C Major Single String

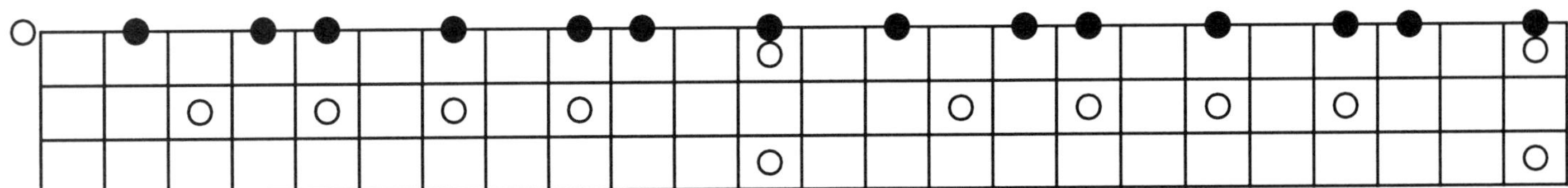

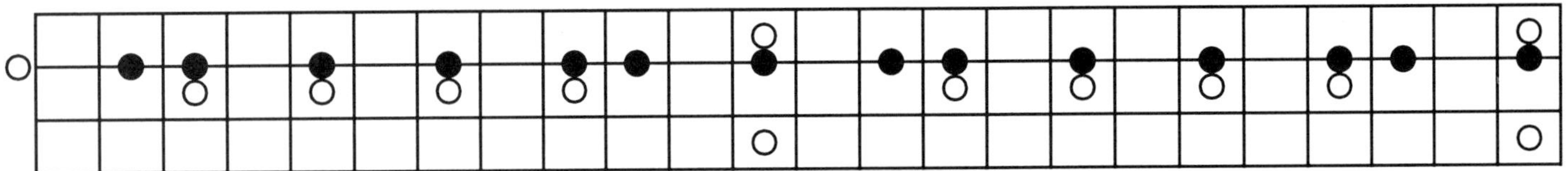

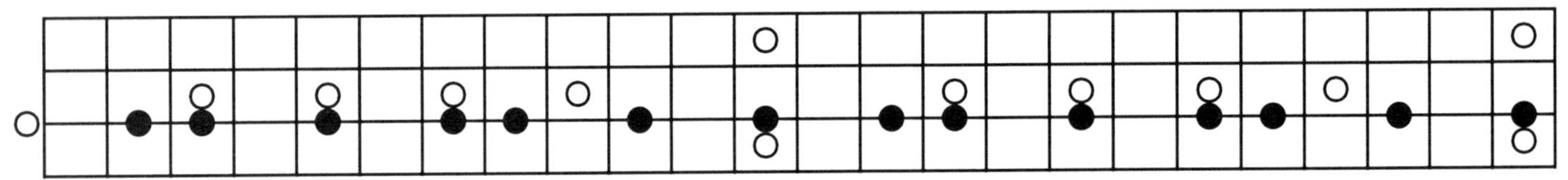

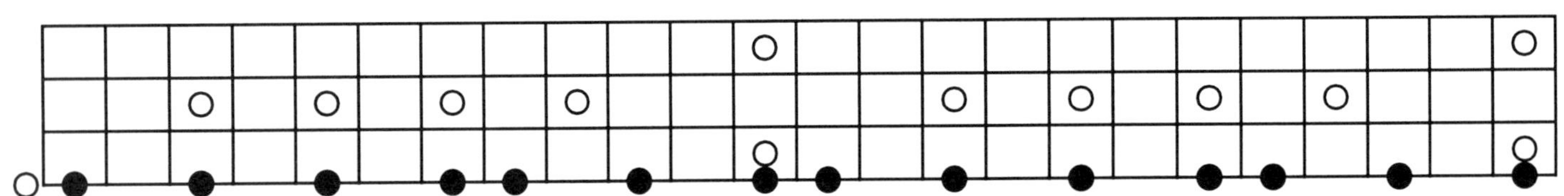

C Major Single String

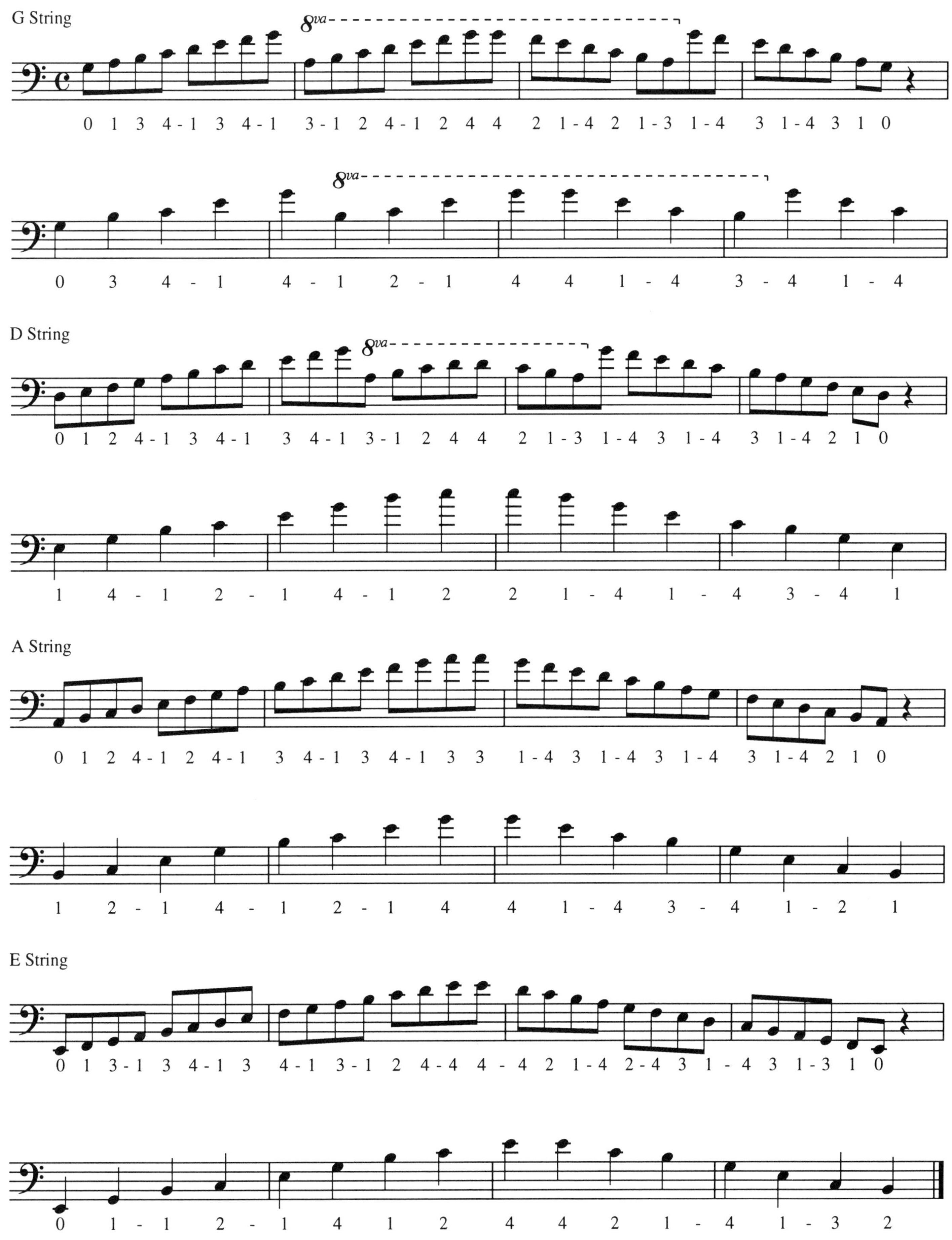

F Major Single String

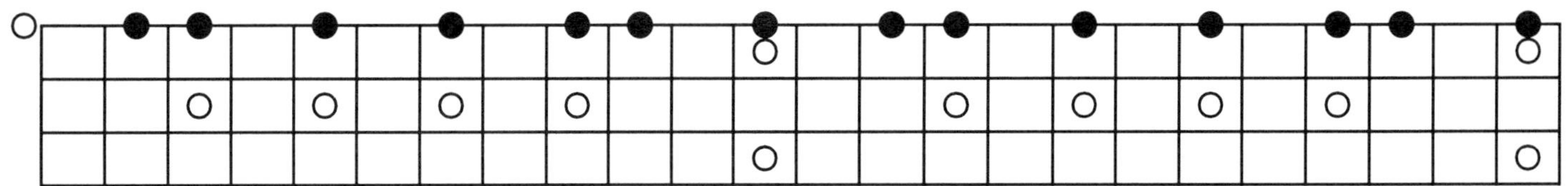

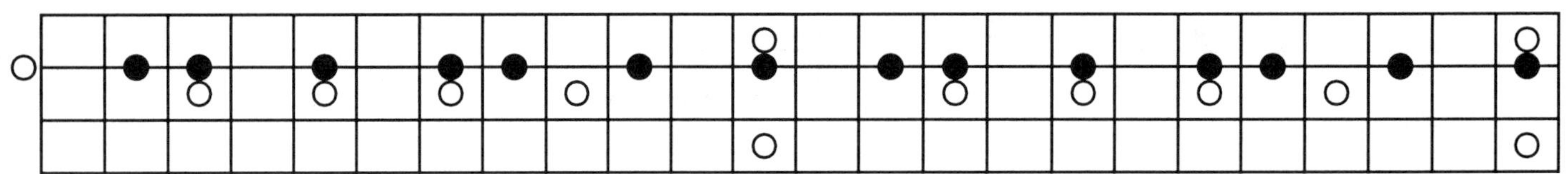

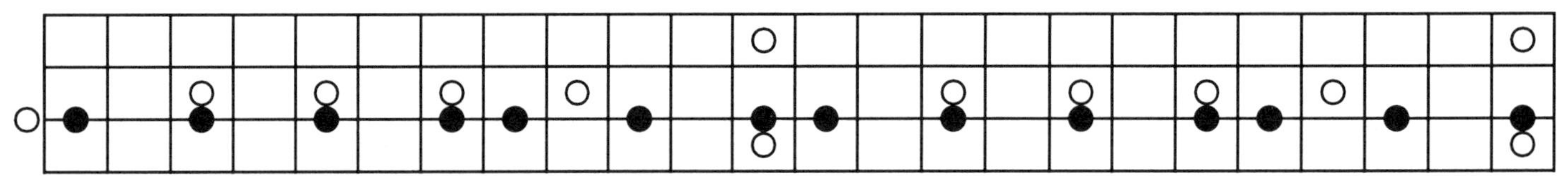

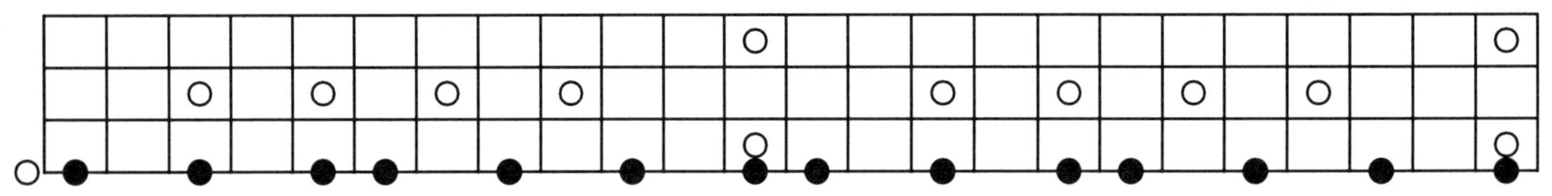

F Major Single String

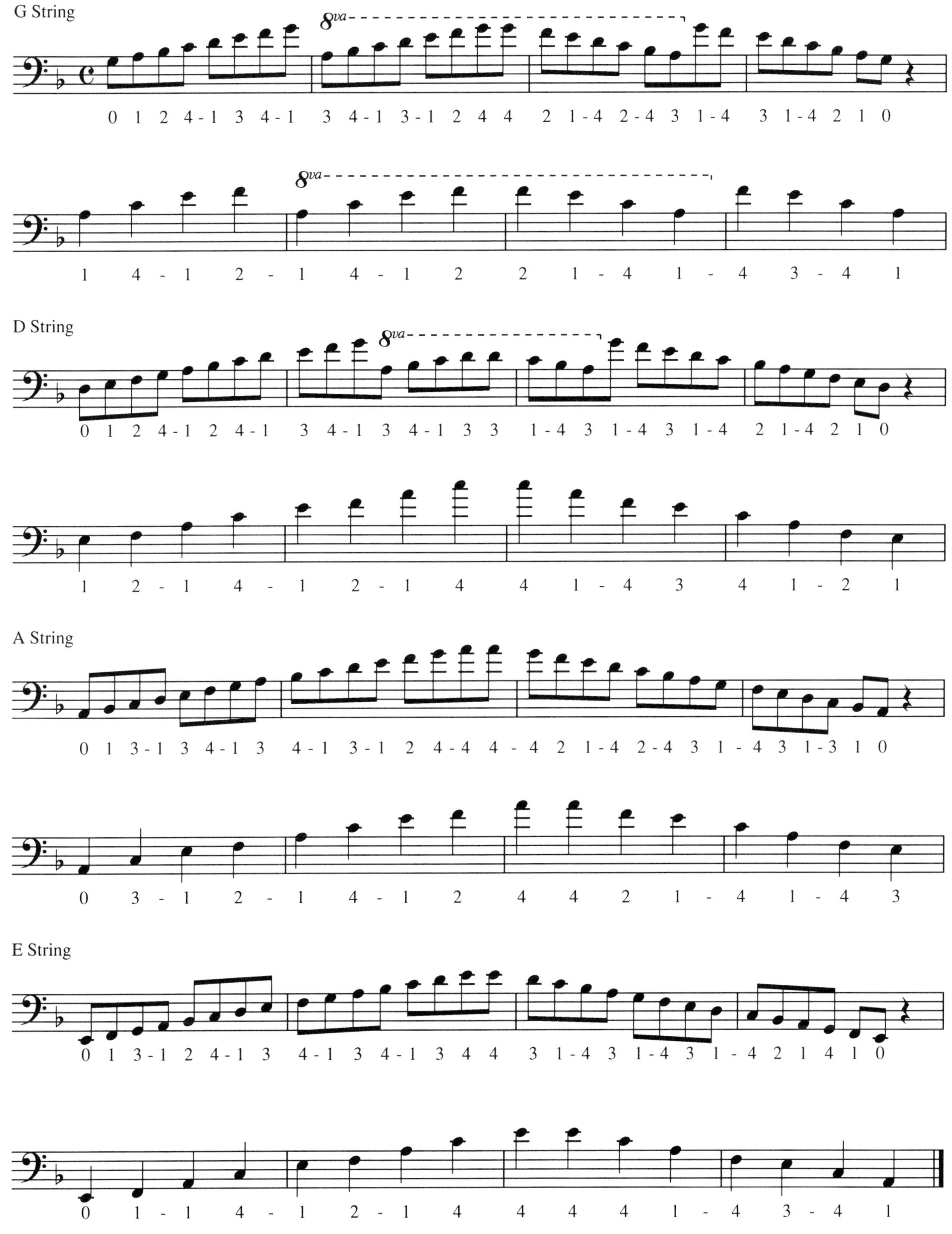

B♭ Major Single String

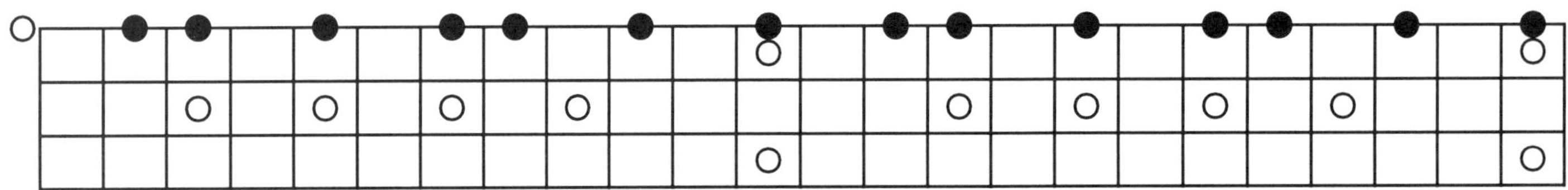

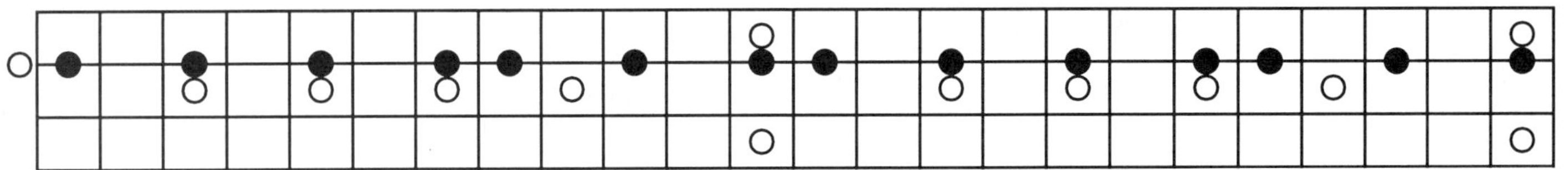

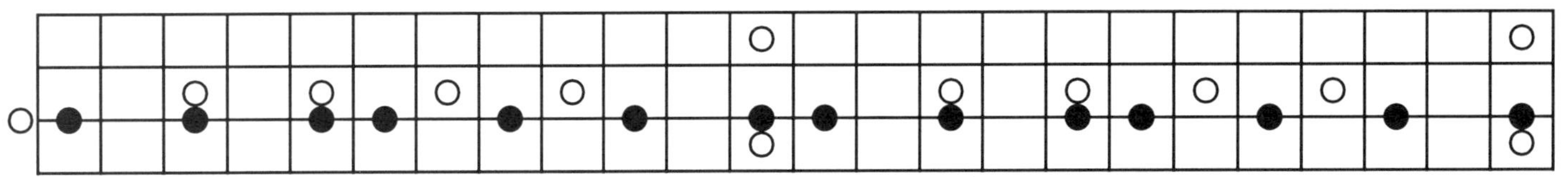

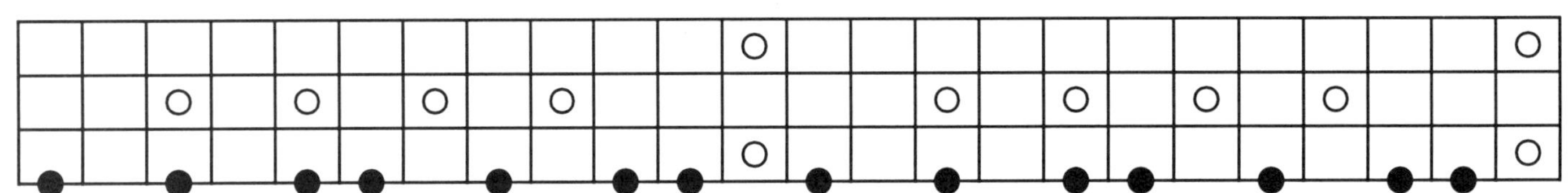

B♭ Major Single String

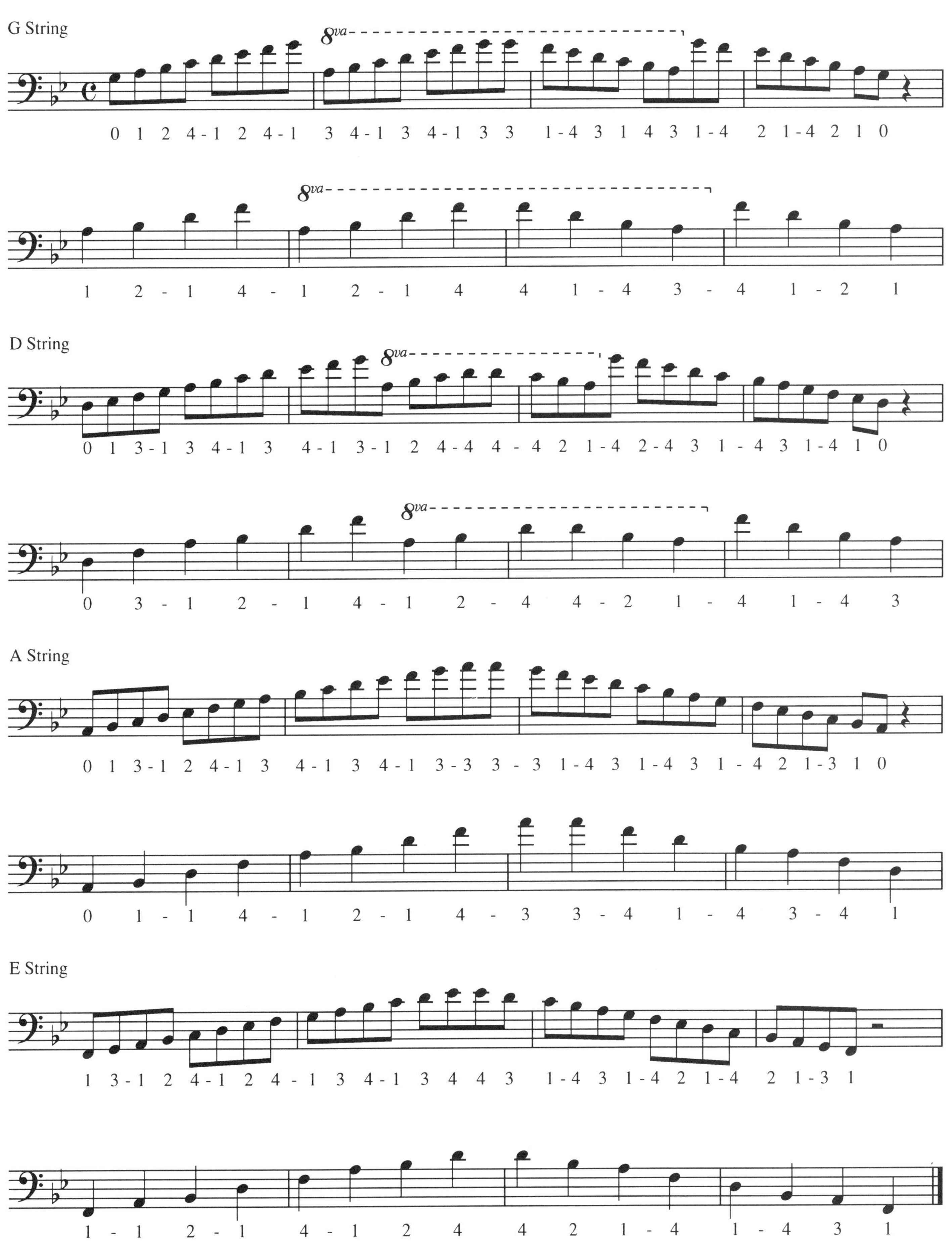

E♭ Major Single String

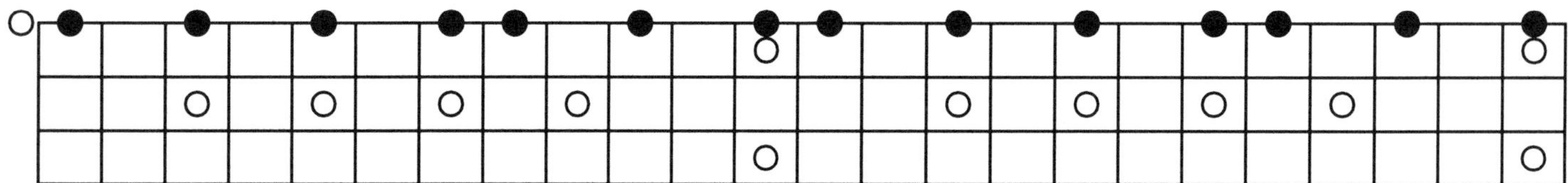

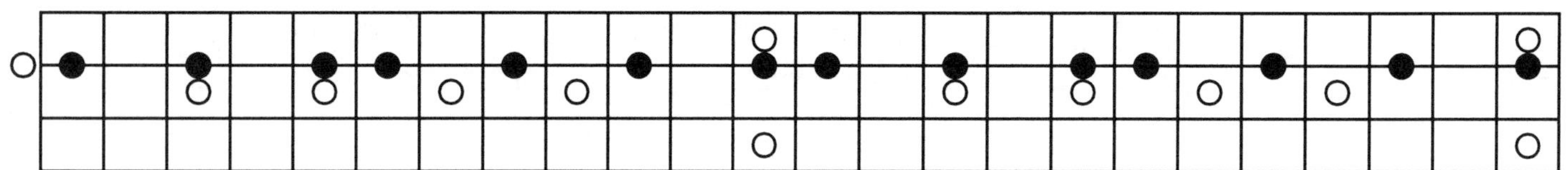

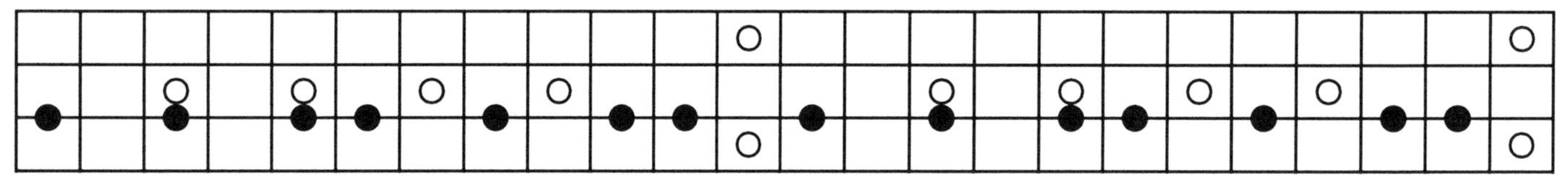

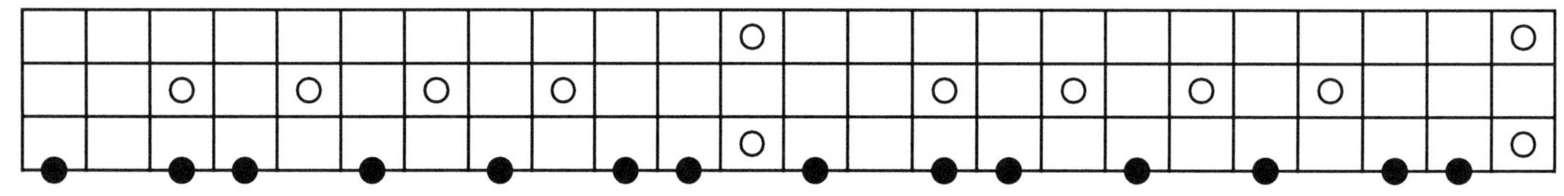

E♭ Major Single String

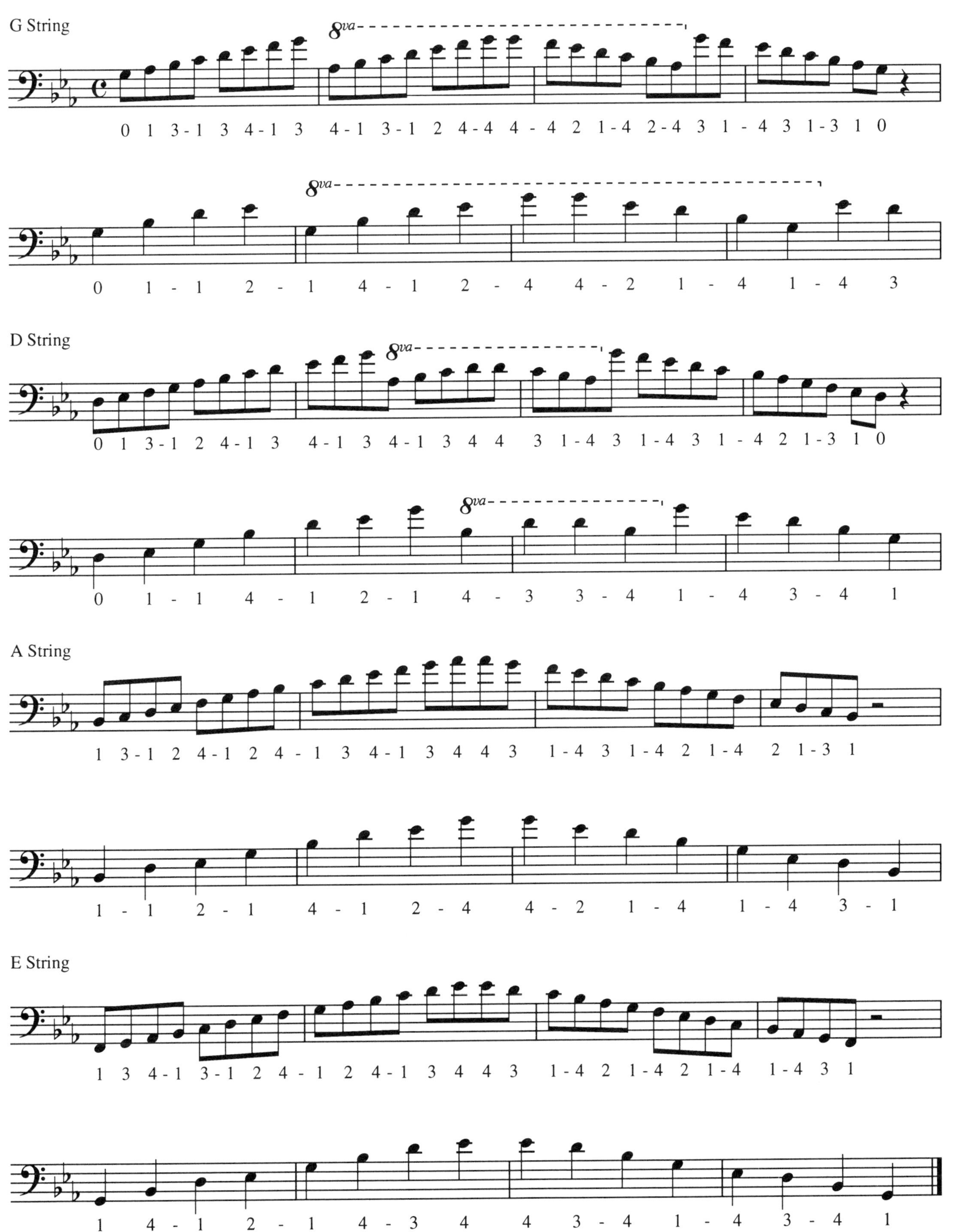

A♭ Major Single String

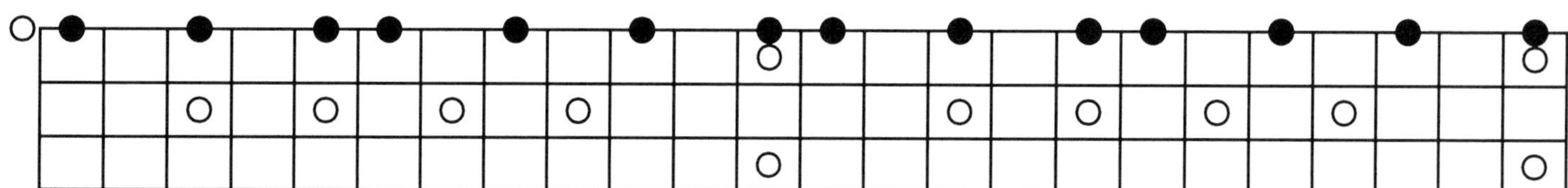

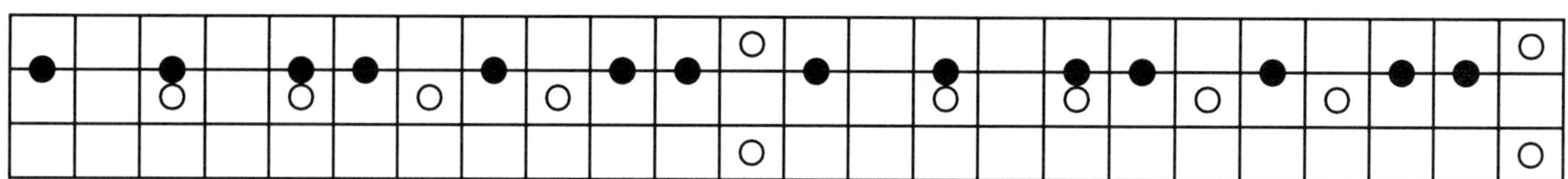

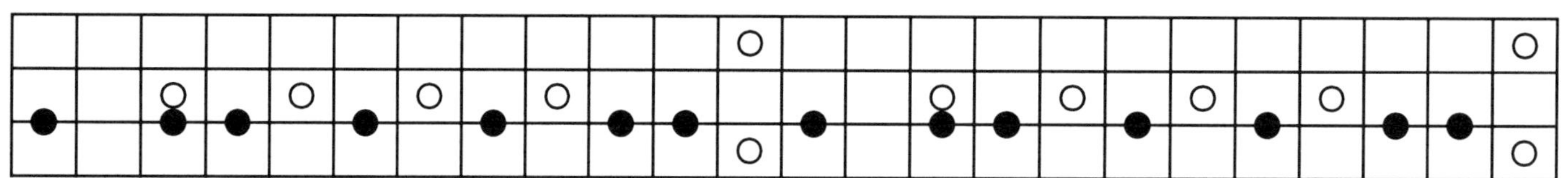

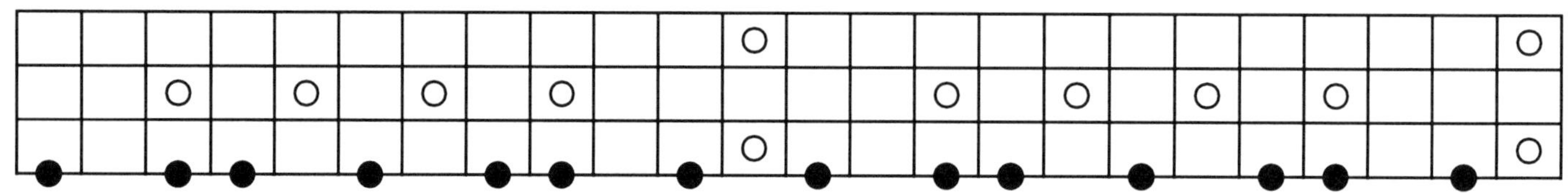

A♭ Major Single String

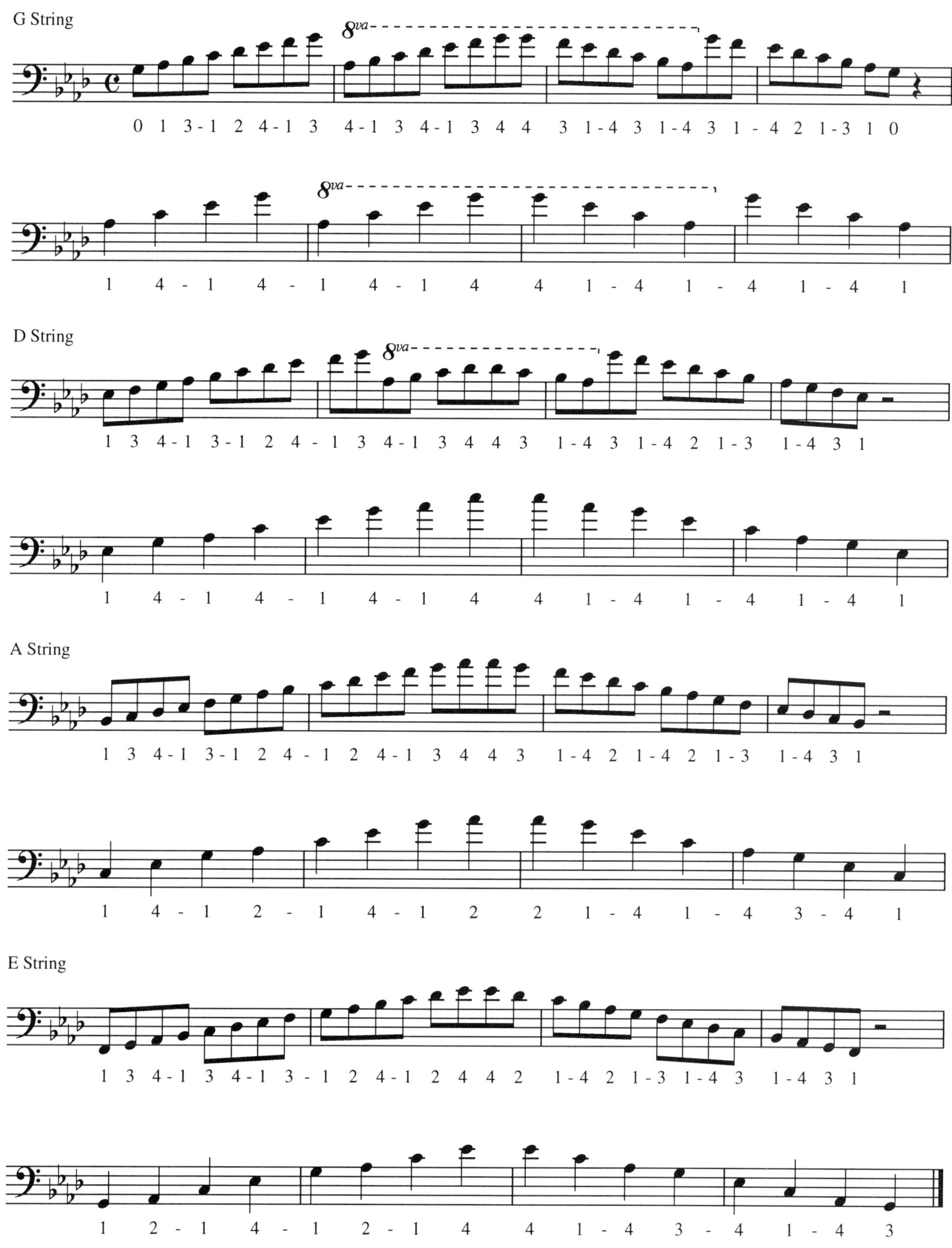

D♭/C♯ Major Single String

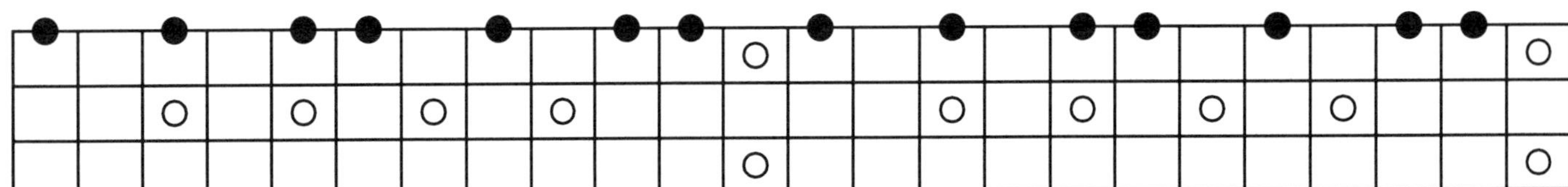

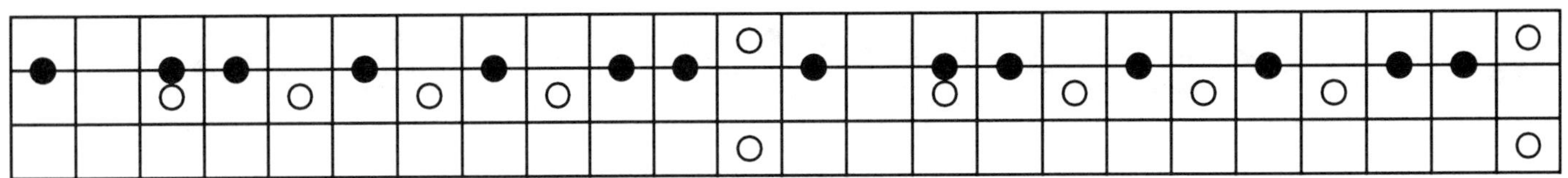

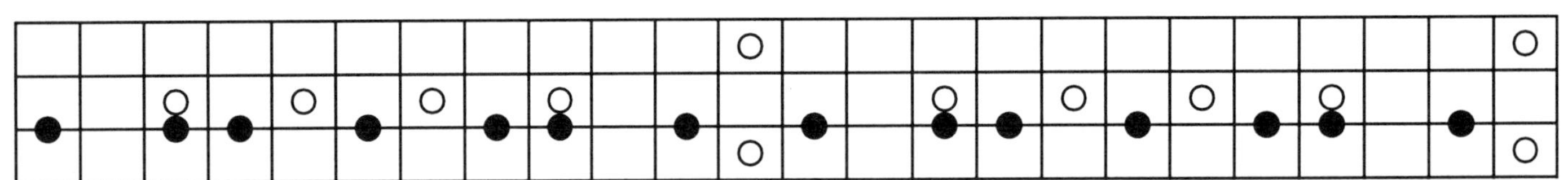

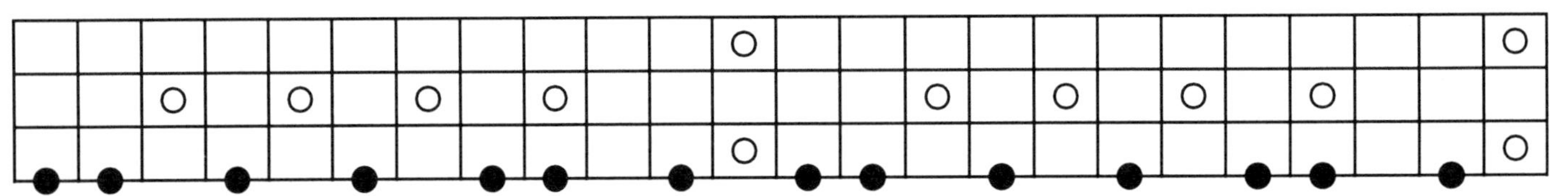

D♭ Major Single String

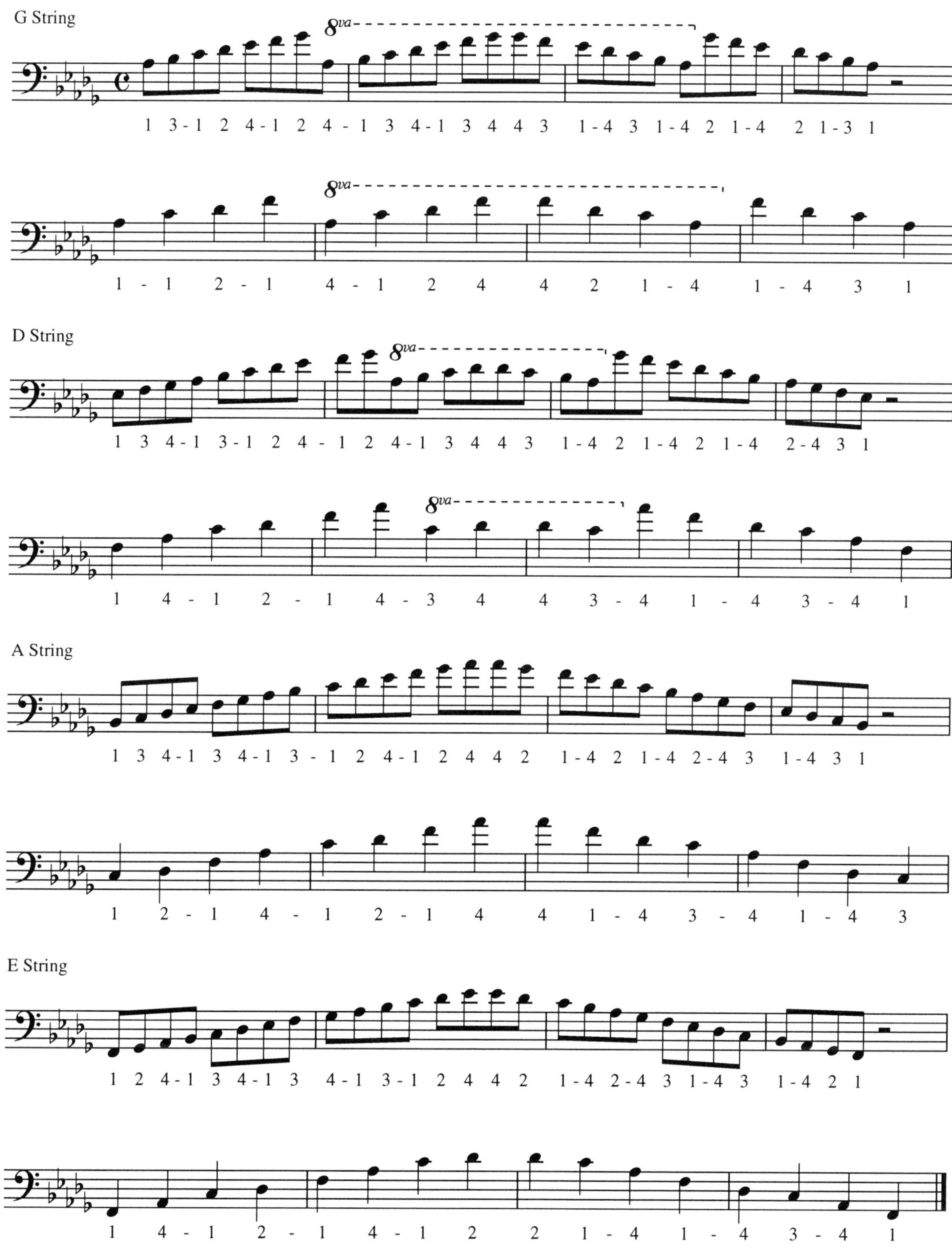

C♯ Major Single String

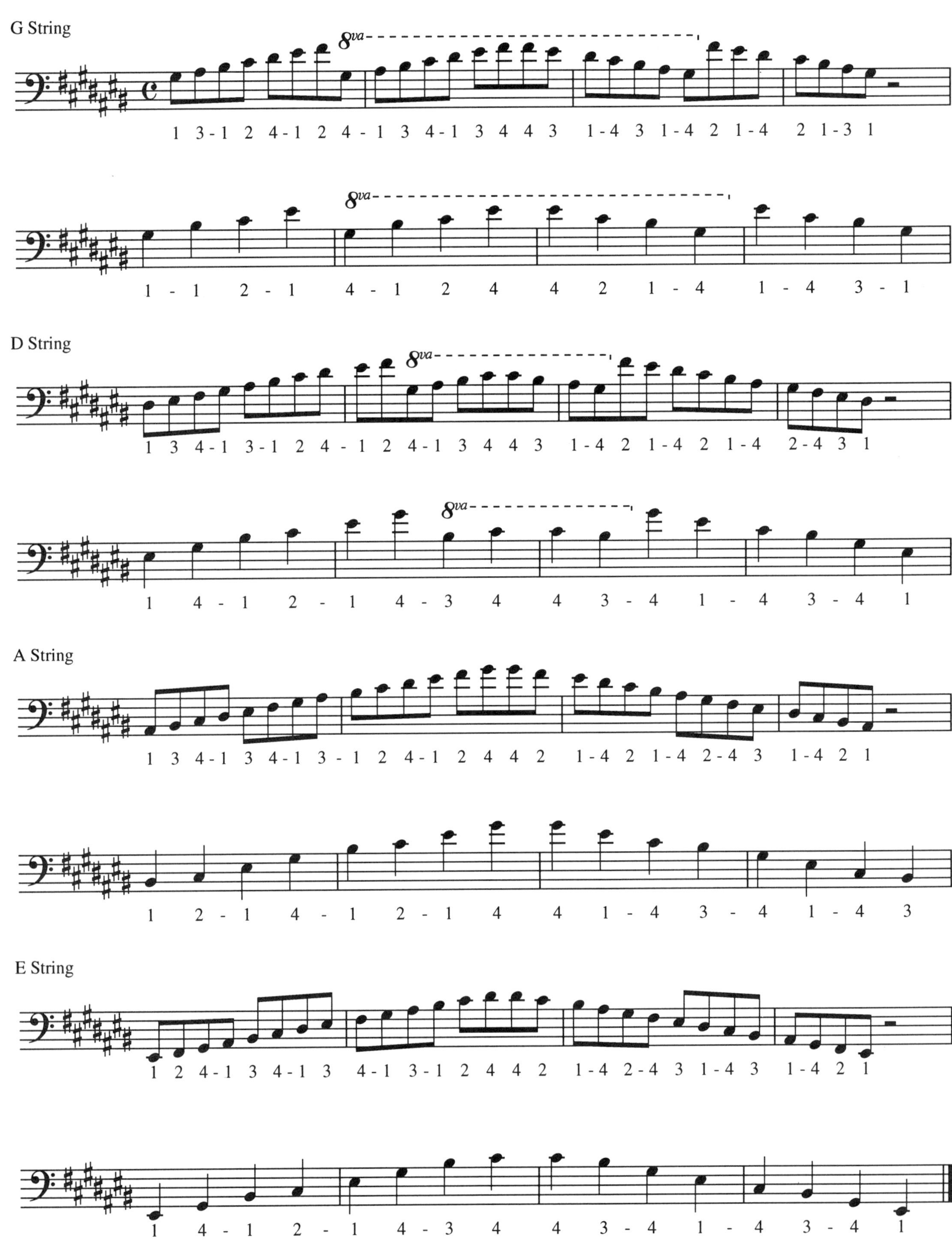

G♭/F♯ Major Single String

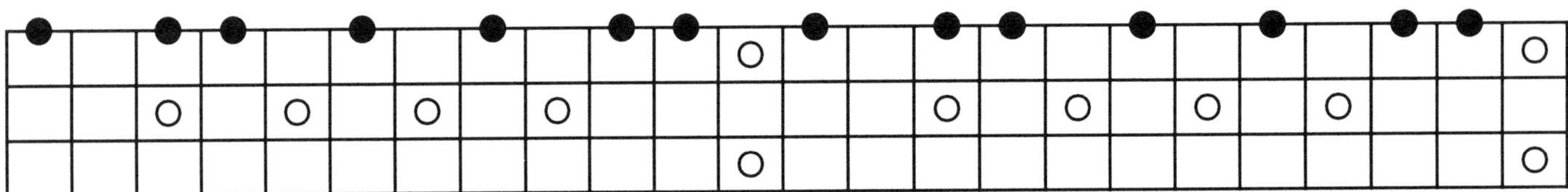

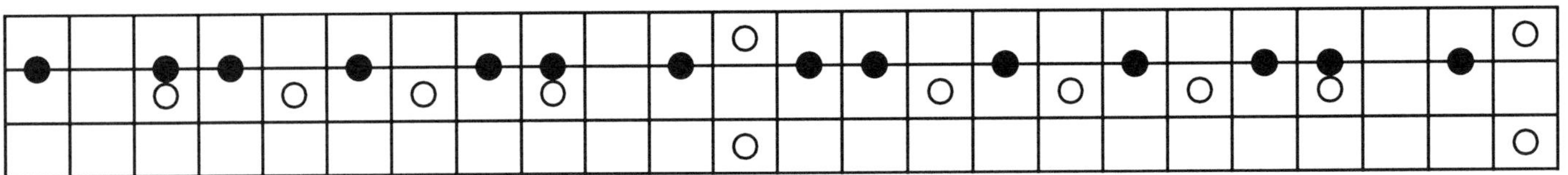

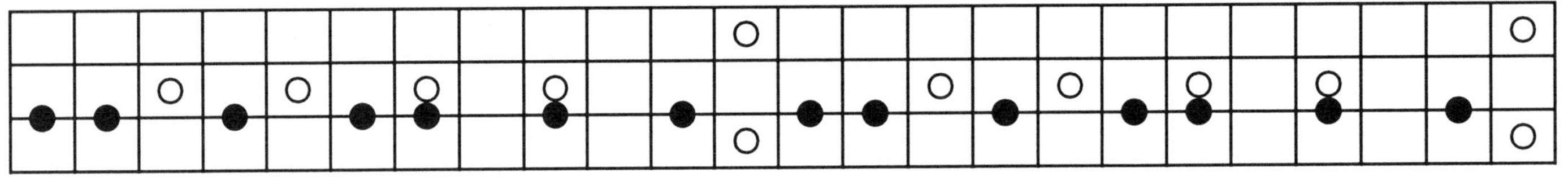

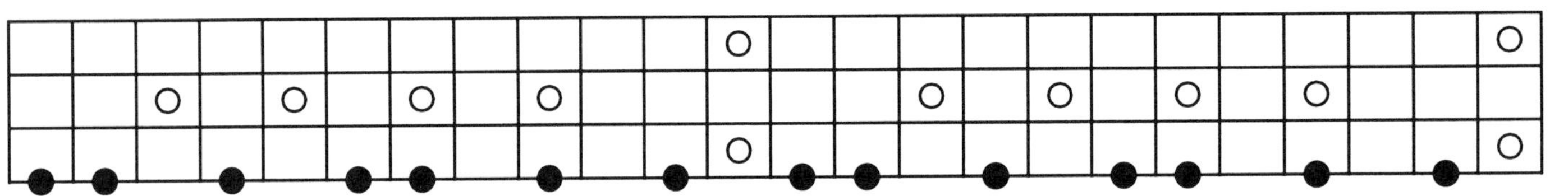

G♭ Major Single String

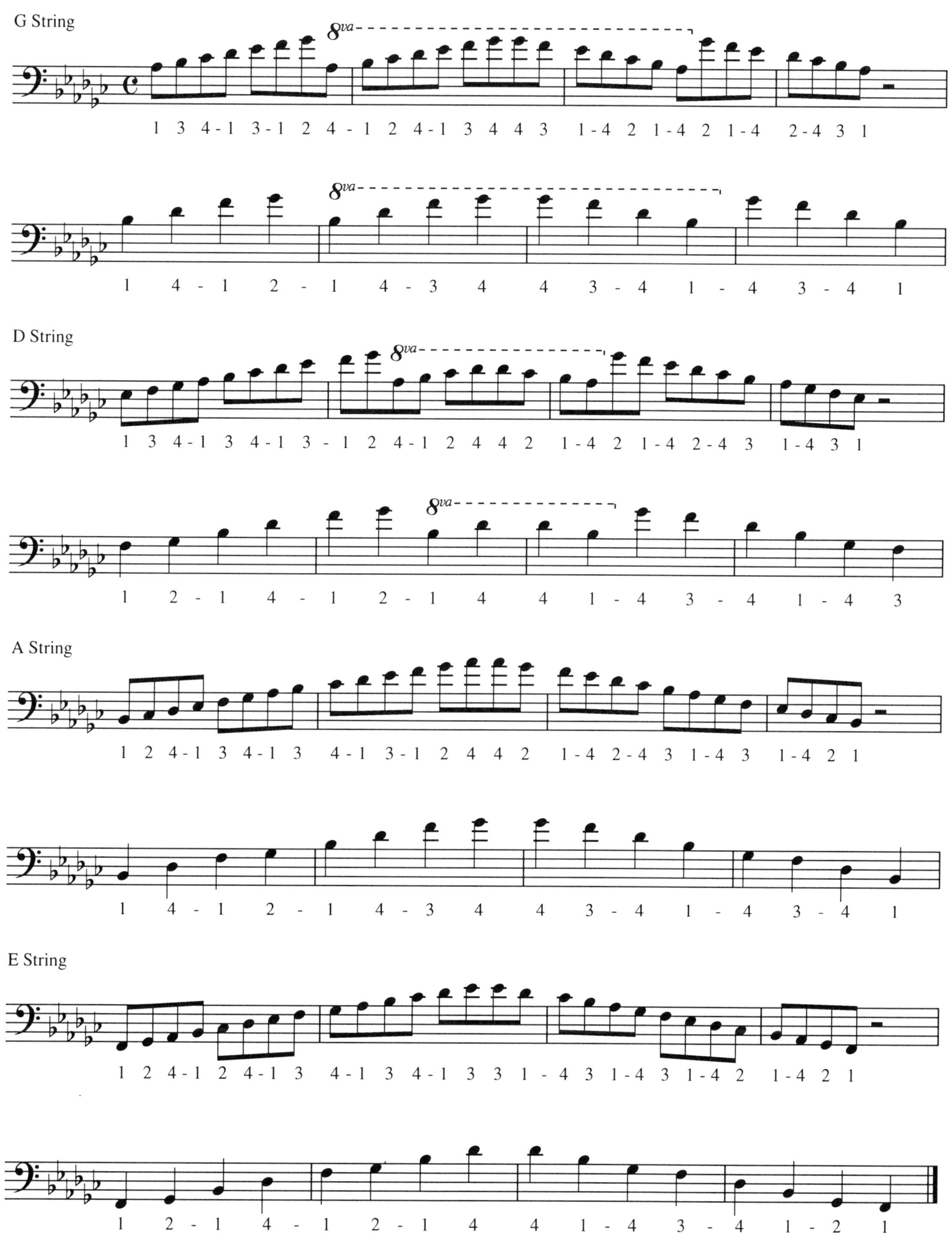

F♯ Major Single String

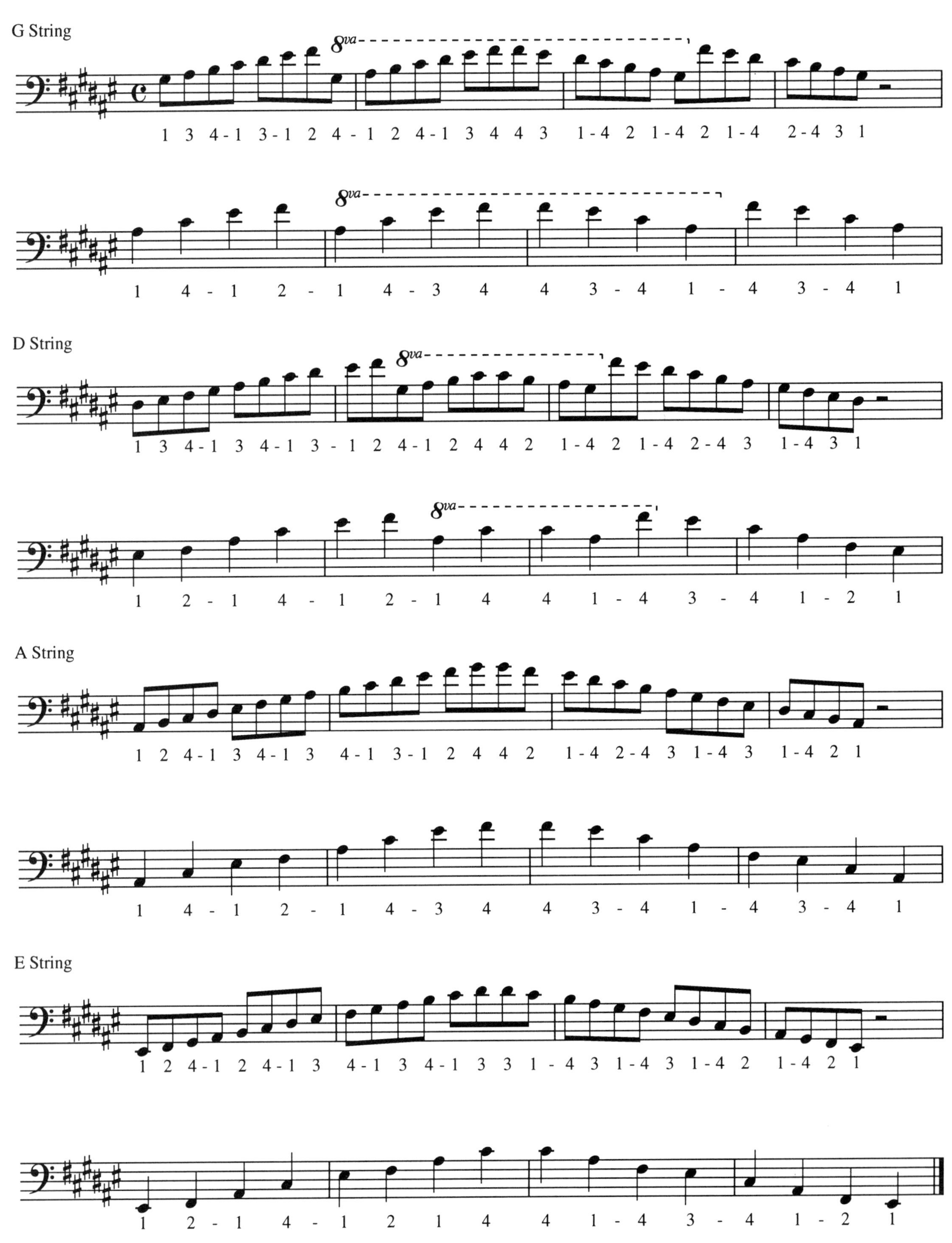

C♭/B Major Single String

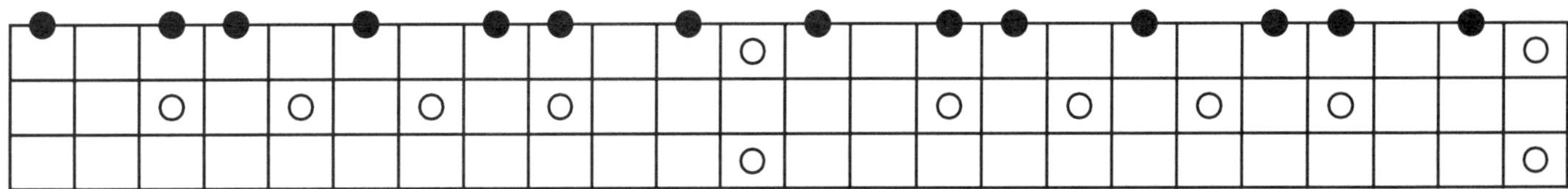

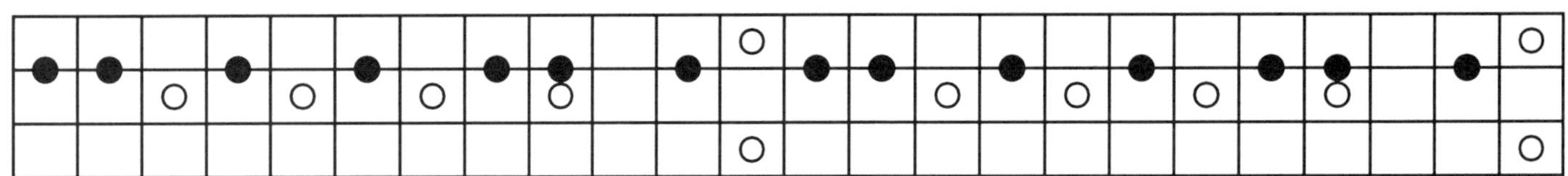

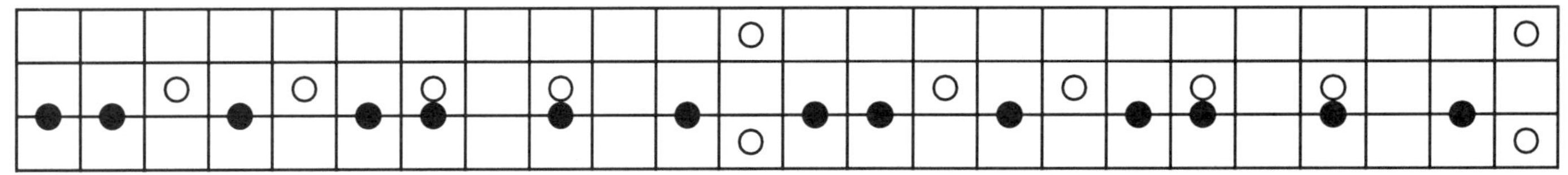

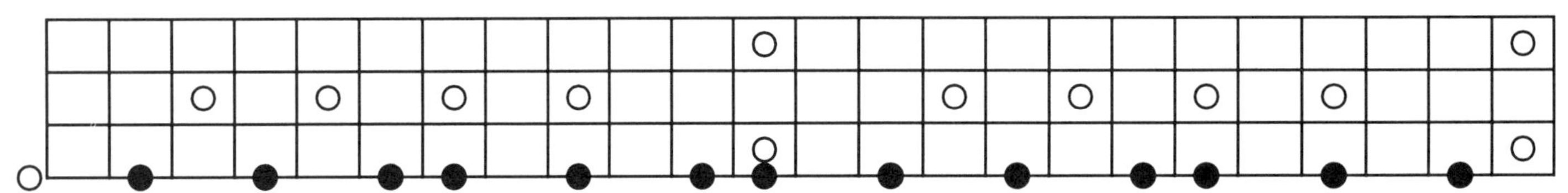

C♭ Major Single String

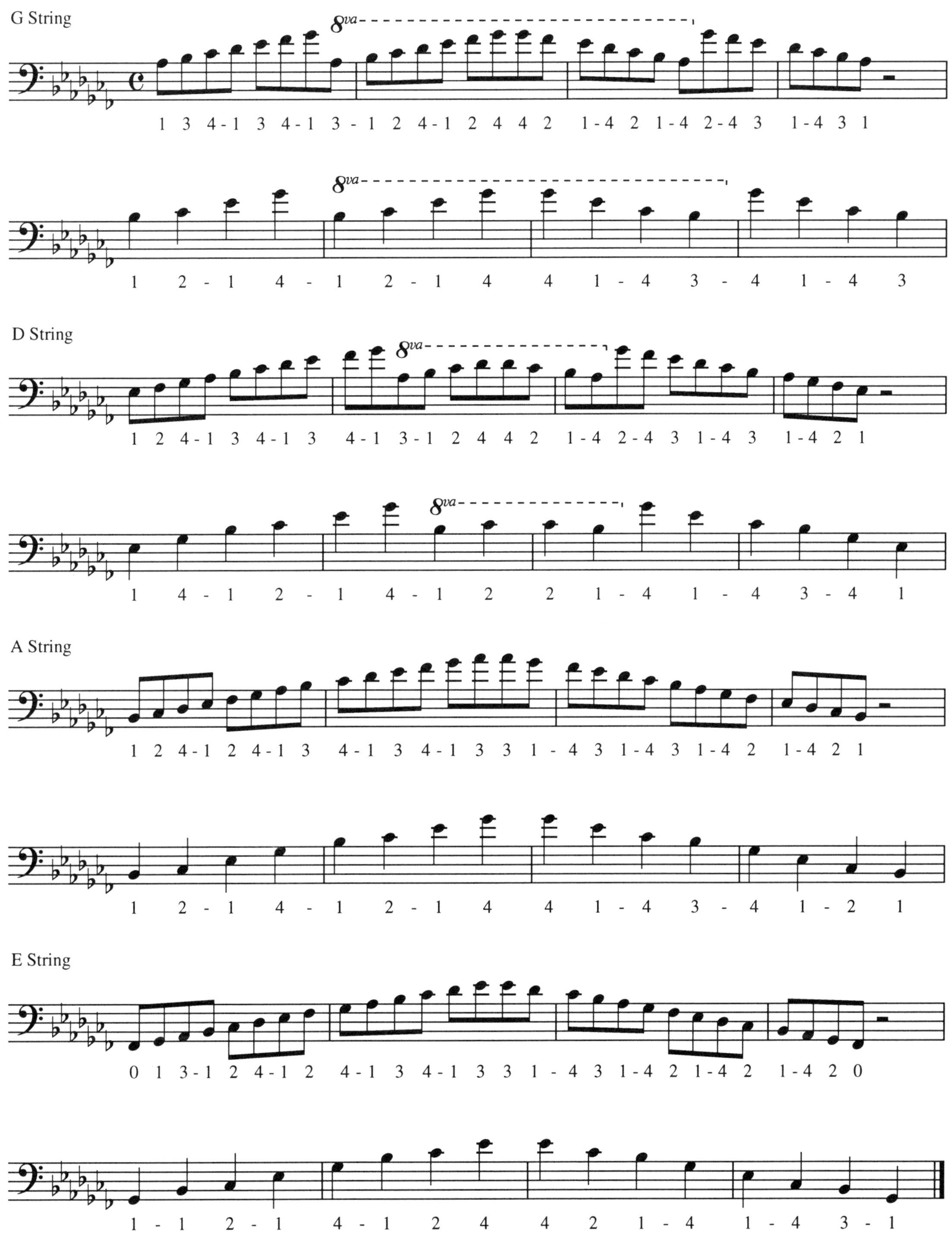

B Major Single String

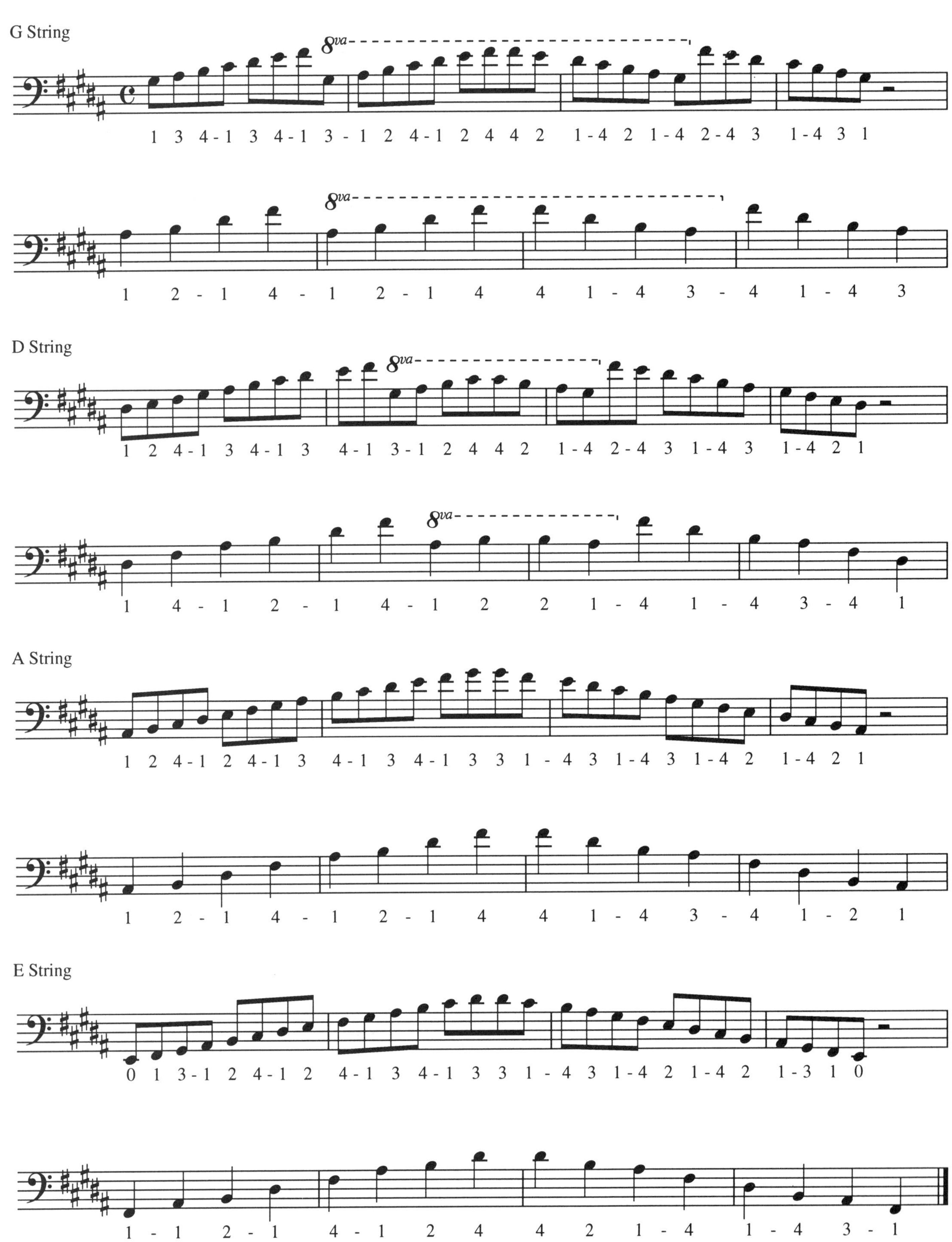

E Major Single String

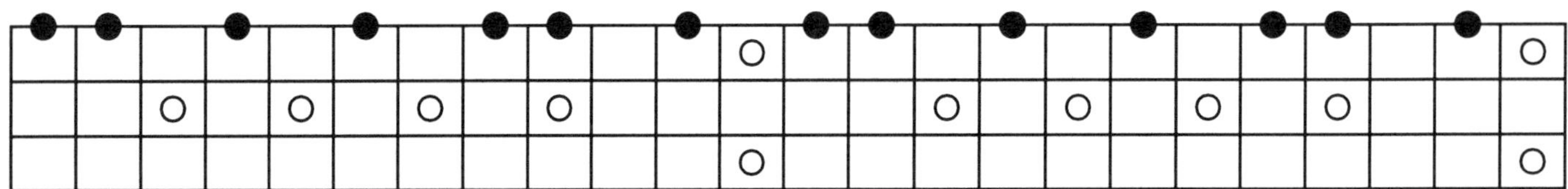

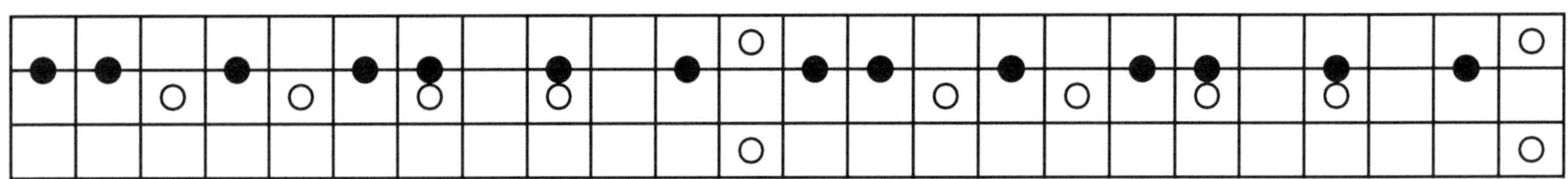

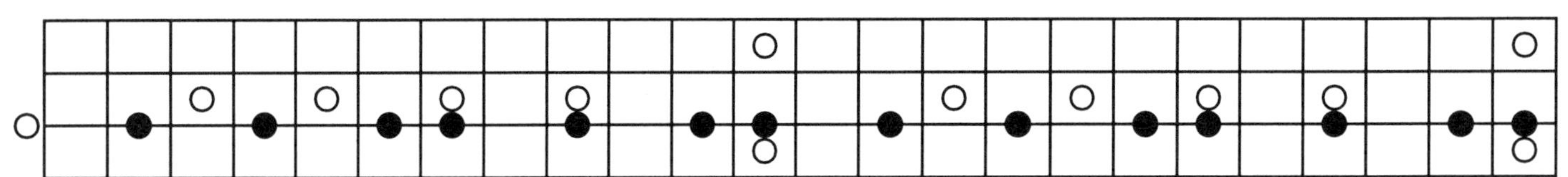

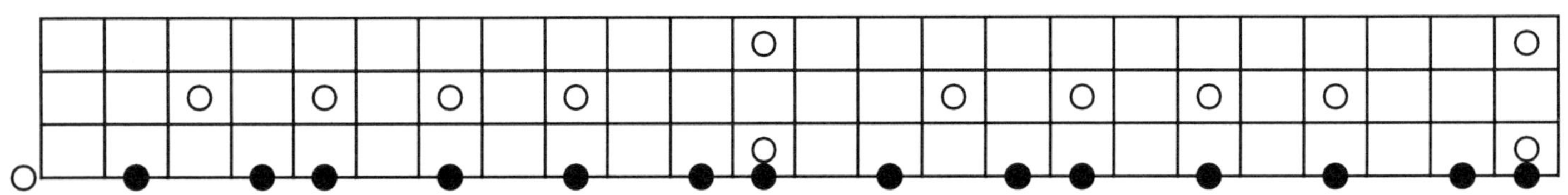

E Major Single String

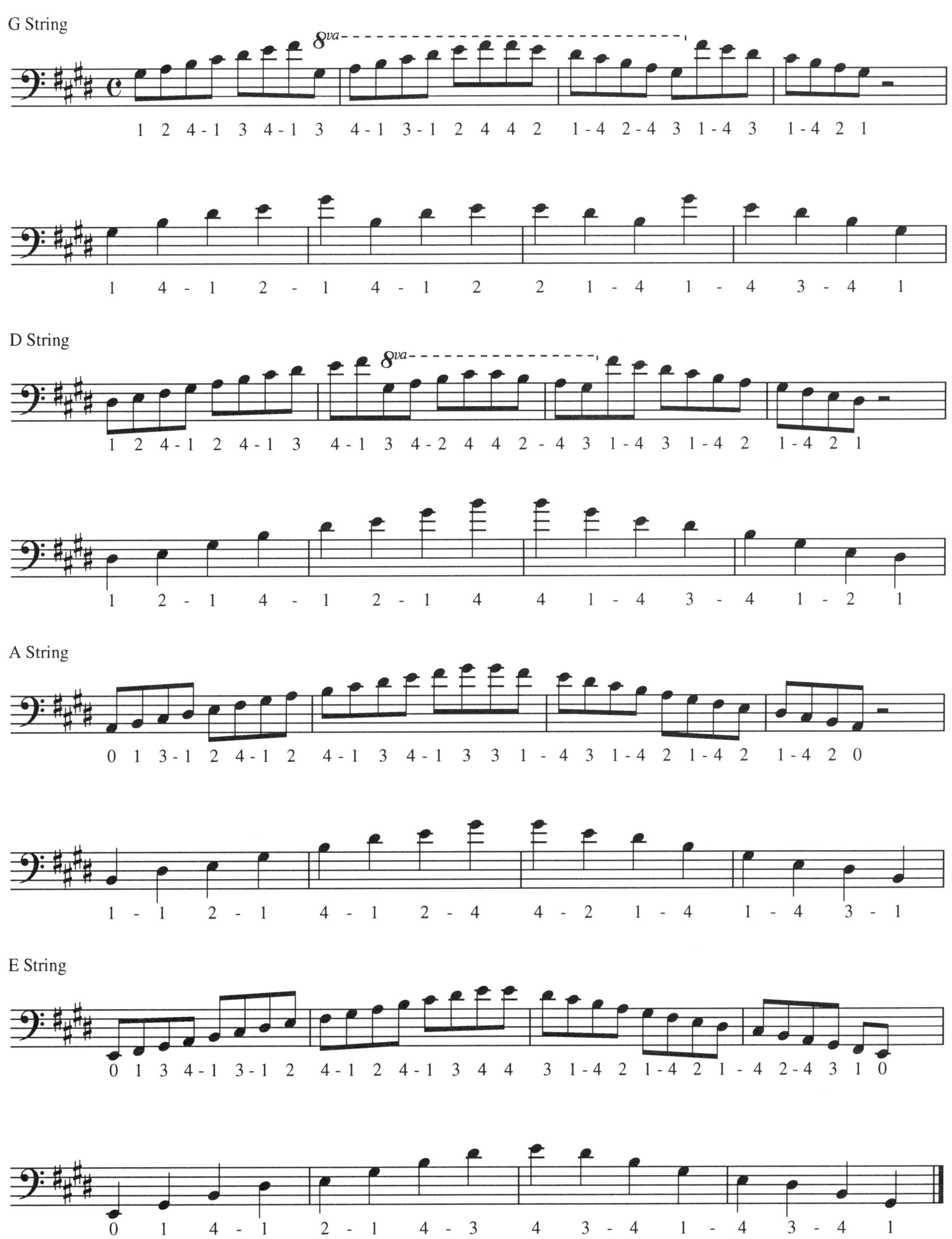

A Major Single String

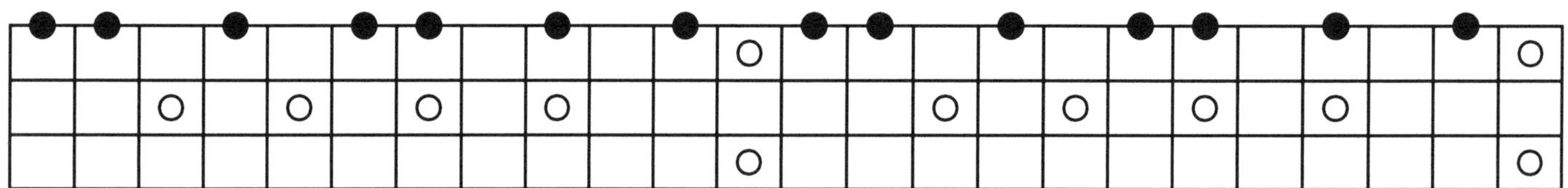

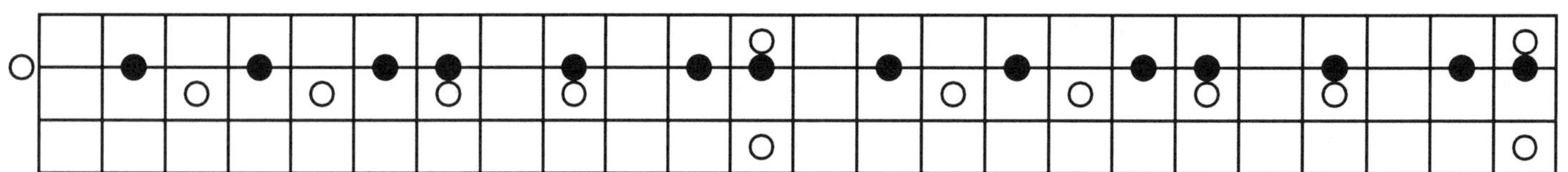

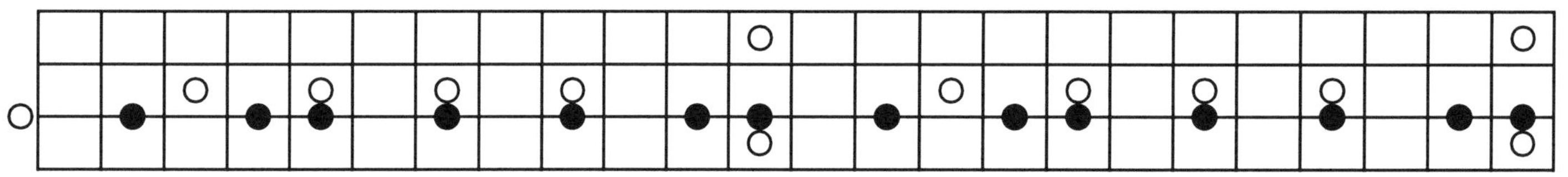

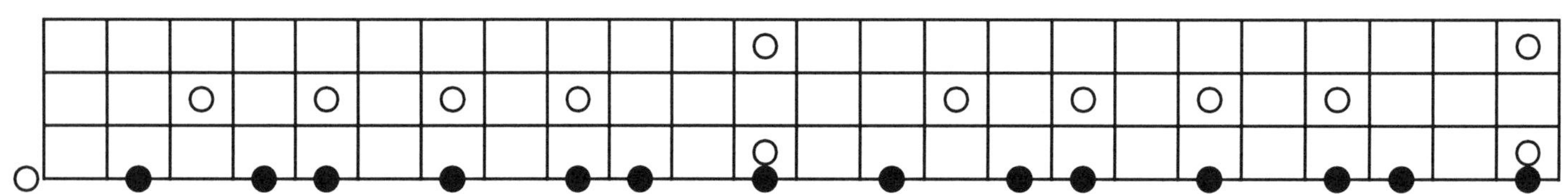

A Major Single String

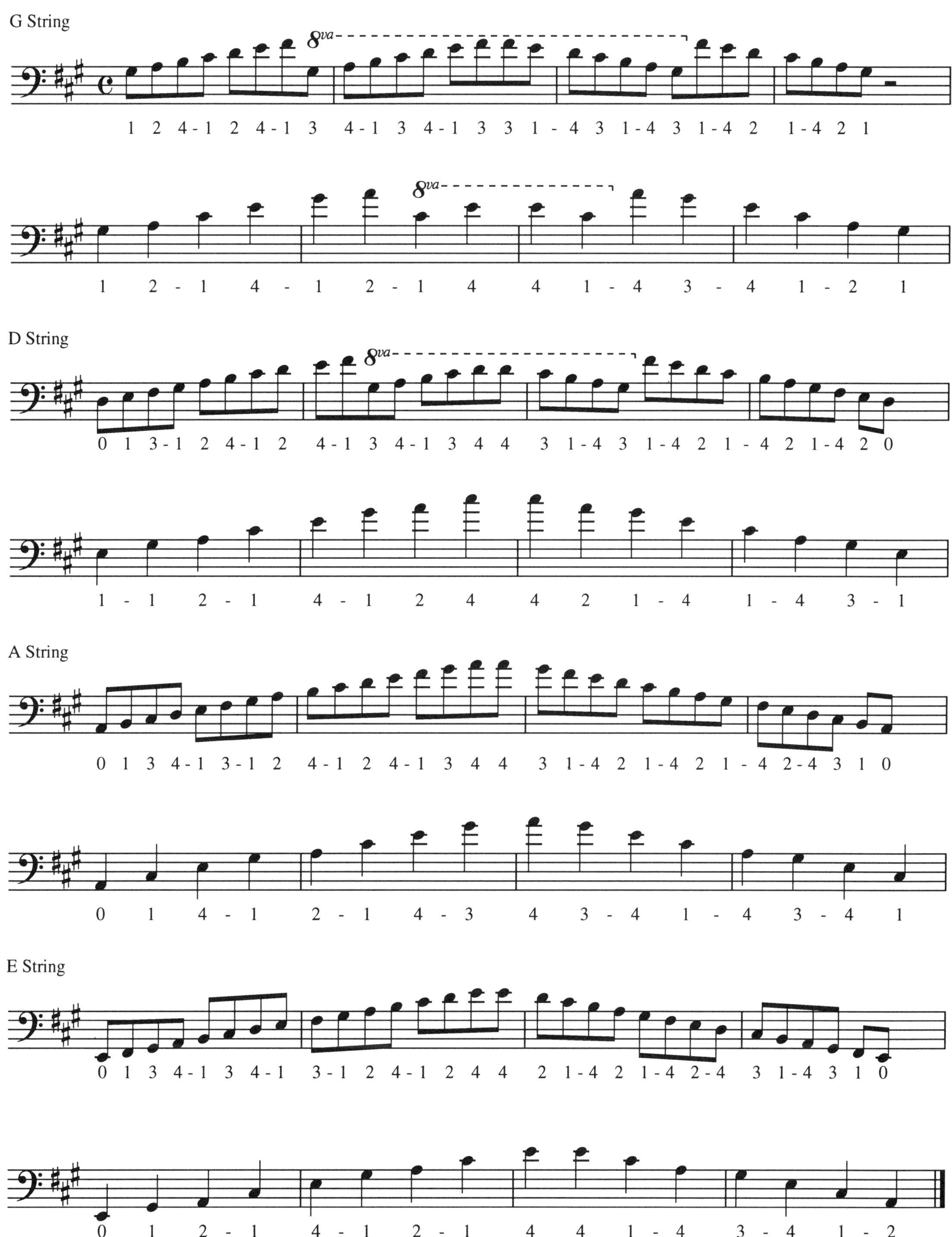

D Major Single String

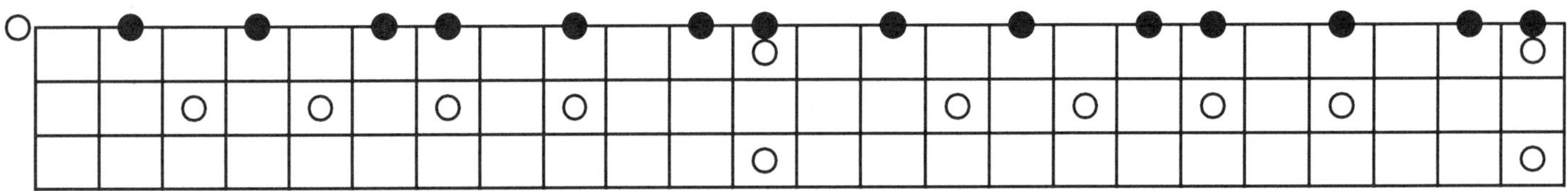

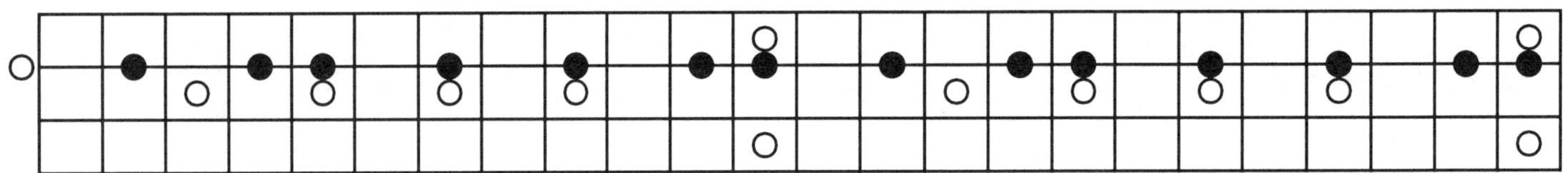

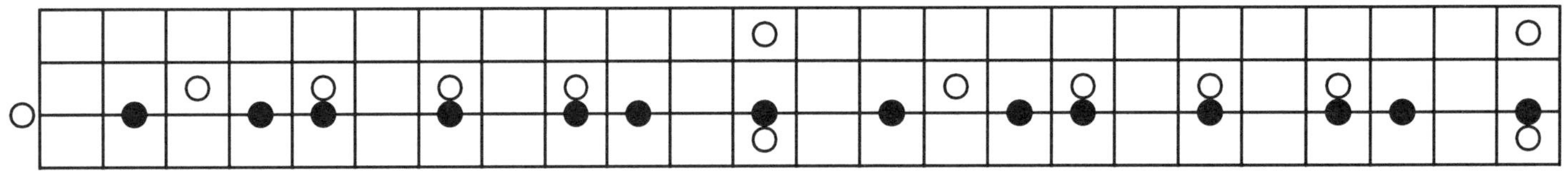

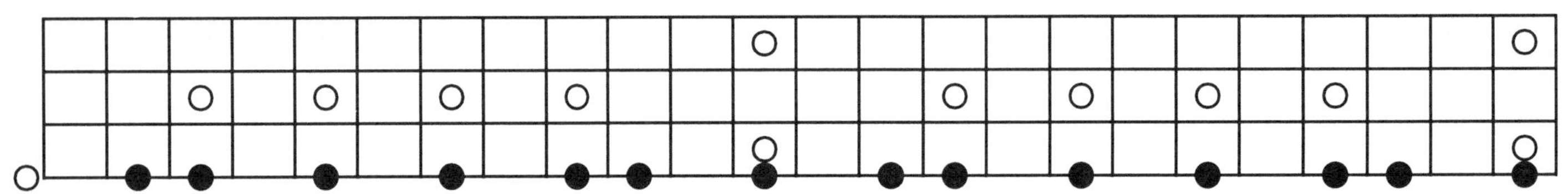

D Major Single String

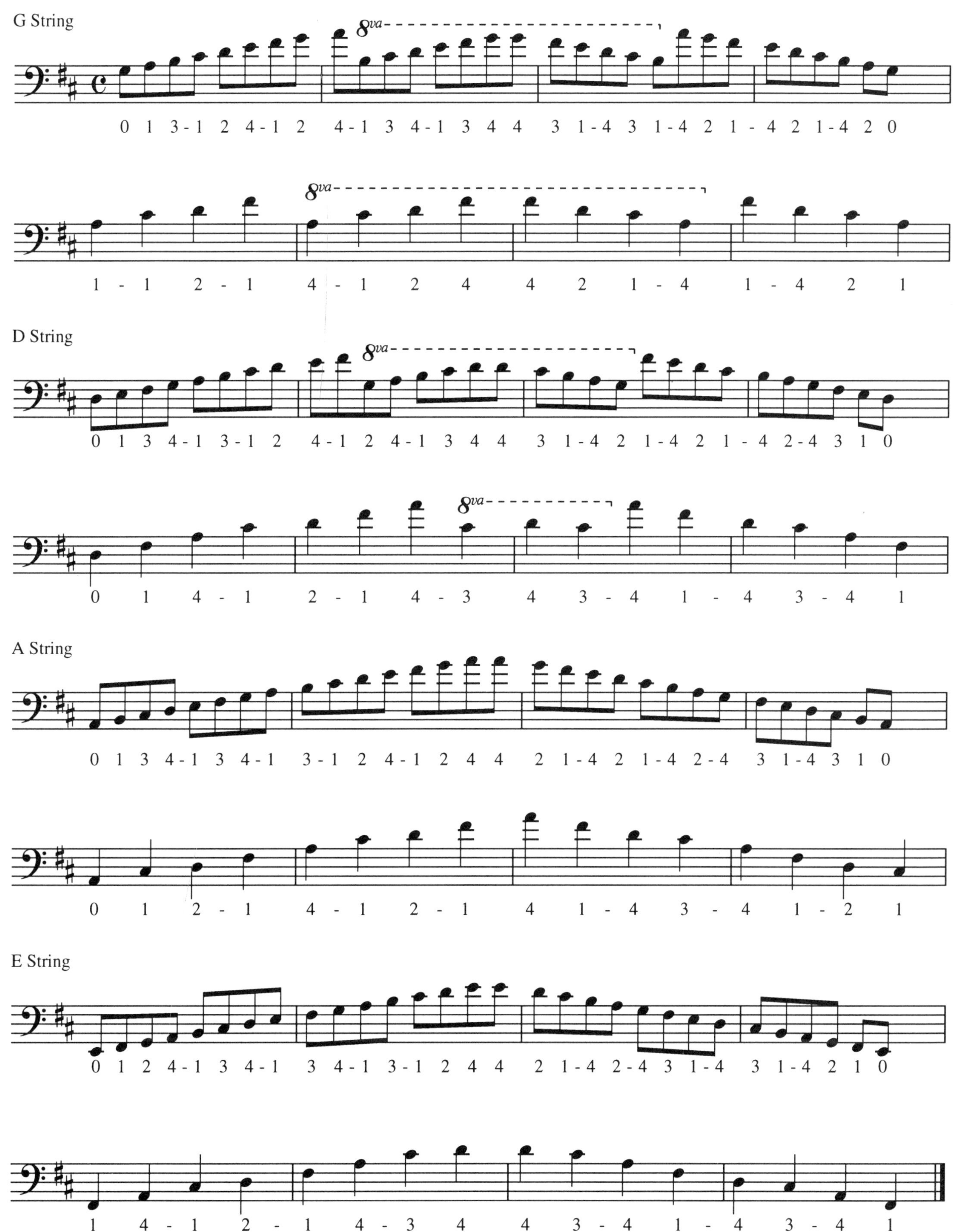

G Major Single String

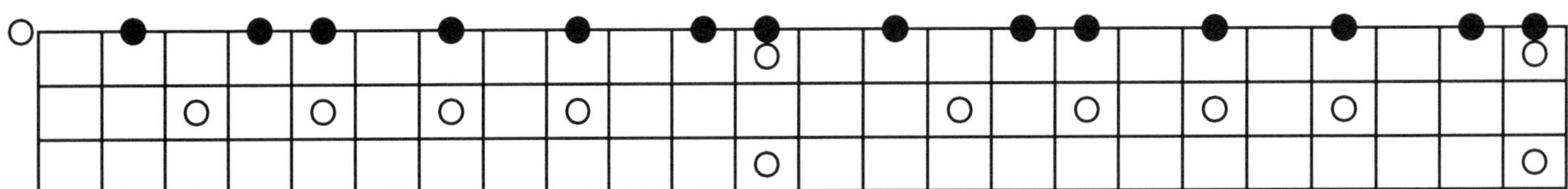

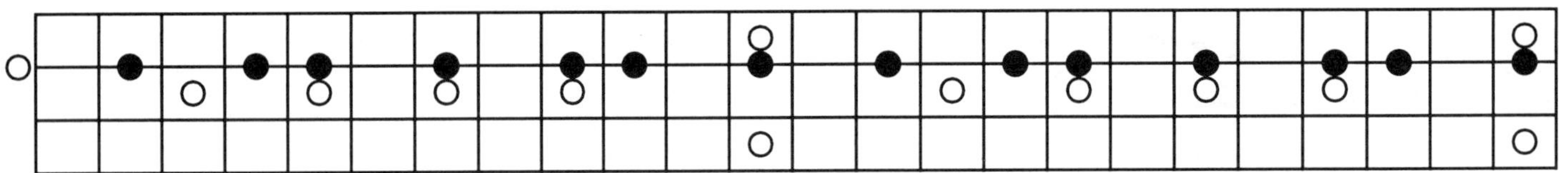

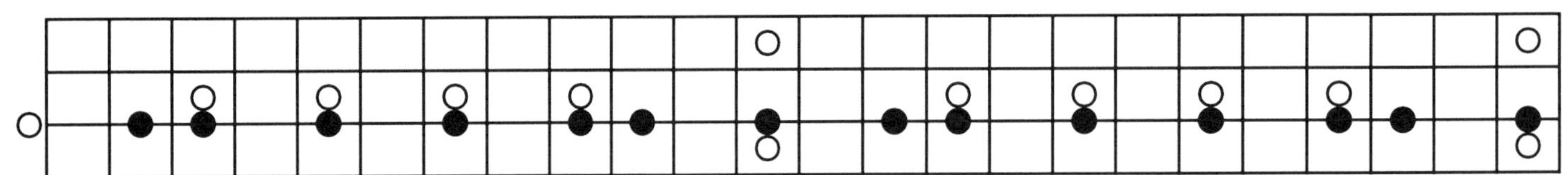

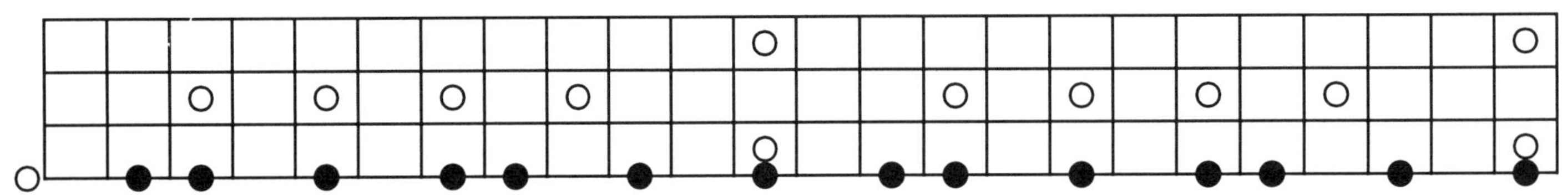

G Major Single String

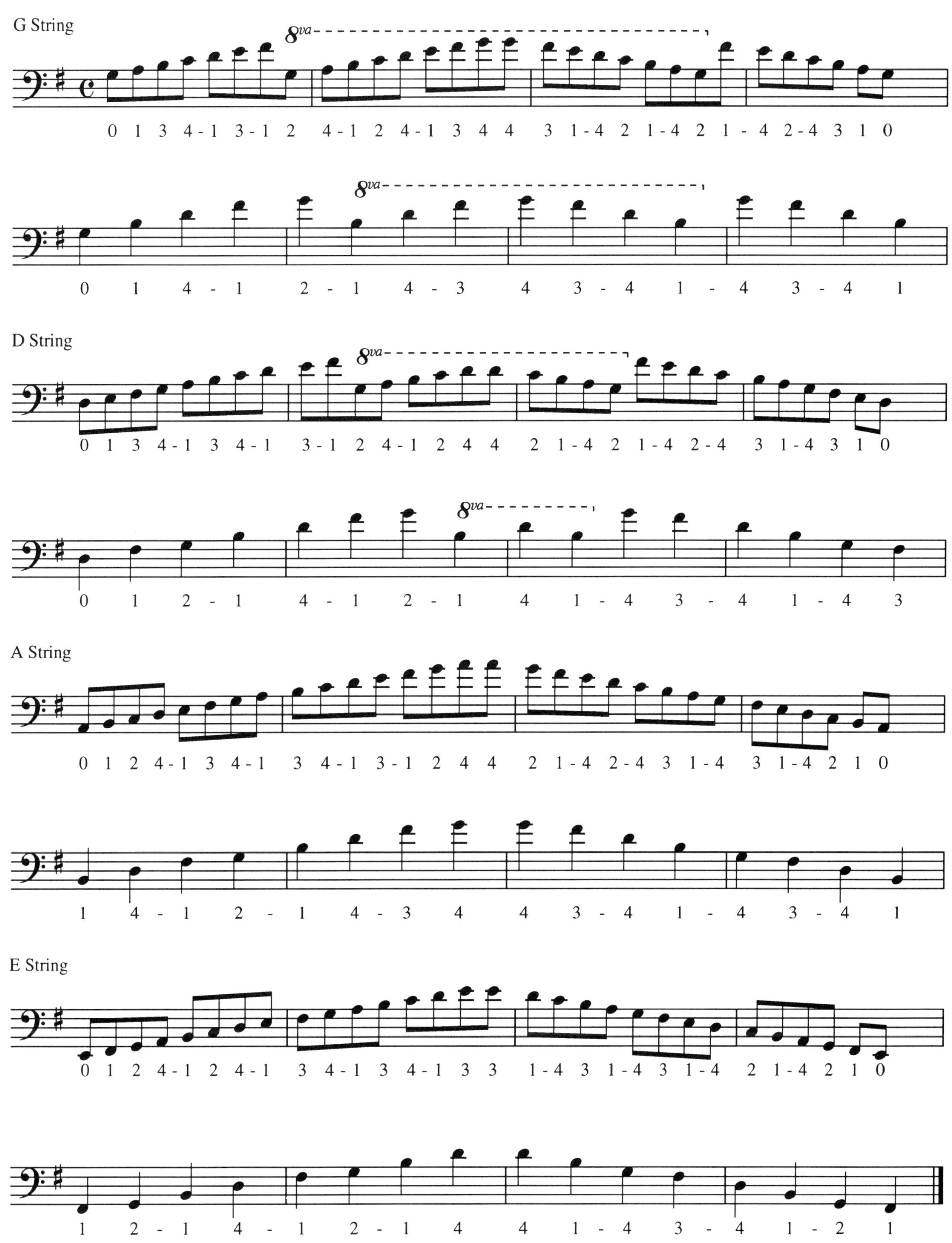

Full Major Scales / Entire Neck

Okay last but not least is the moment we've all been waiting for! By combining all of the past exercises in this book, you should be able to complete this last chapter pretty easily although it might take a lifetime to master.

Now that you've done all of the scale and arpeggio studies in different positions along the neck as well as up and down each string, this next exercise is all up to you. What you want to do is to be able to play each major scale and arpeggio up and down the entire neck starting with the lowest note available on your E string, to the highest note available on your G string. Of course the highest note depends on how many frets you have on your bass. If you have a 24 fret bass the highest note will be G. If you've got a 20 fret P Bass, the highest note will be E flat. It all depends on your bass.

I've written out each major scale starting with the lowest note available on your E string all the way up to high G on your 24th fret on you G string if you have it available. Notice I did not include any fingerings. This is where it's all up to you. The reason being is that there are so many possibilities that for me to list them all here in this book would be crazy. Besides, this is where you get to explore all of the different avenues for each major scale up and down your neck. I also didn't include the arpeggio notation because you should know the notes of each arpeggio for each respective scale by now. On the neck chart, I did include four very different possibilities of a C major scale up and down the neck for you to check out. The number of other possibilities is virtually limitless.

Like I said, take this time to really explore your neck in each key. Make sure to practice coming down the neck as well as going up it. Take your time with each key and try to write out some of the avenues and fingerings that you come up with. Don't just play it linear either, you can play studies in thirds, fourths, fifths etc. Be sure to practice the arpeggios too!!!

I hope that this book has been helpful in your journey of learning and becoming a bass player as well as a musician!!! I also hope that you had as much fun learning all of the cool stuff inside as I did writing it!!!!!!

Peace- Dino

Entire Neck Full Major Scales

8va

8va

8va

8va

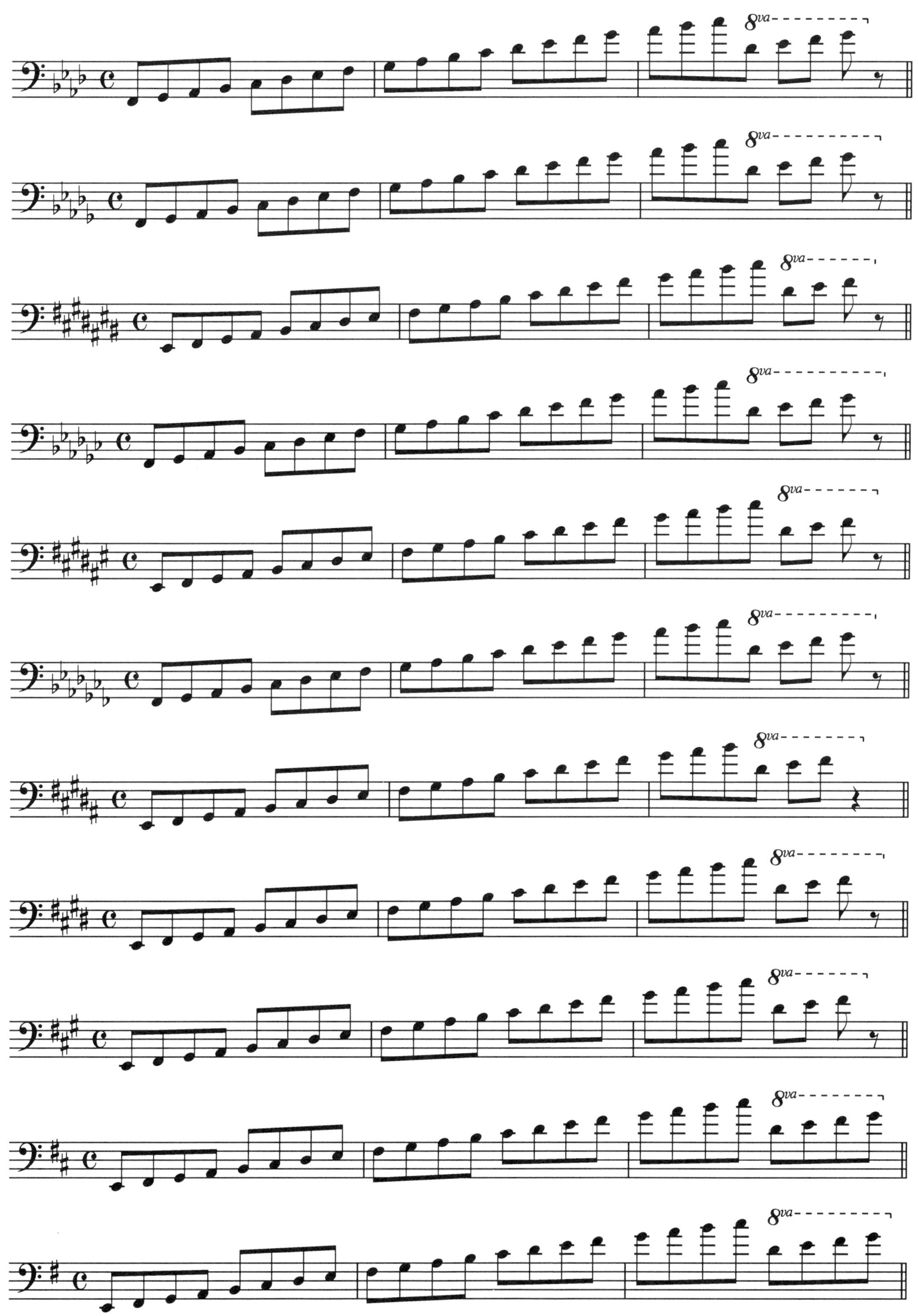

8va
8va
8va
8va
8va
8va
8va
8va
8va
8va
8va

Four Different Possibilities of Complete C Major Scale Up and Down the Neck

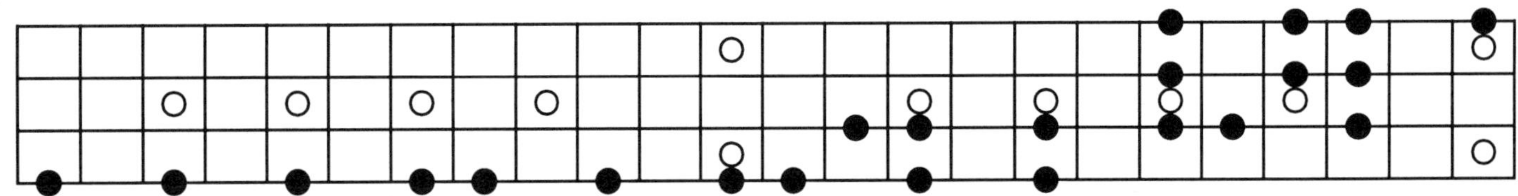

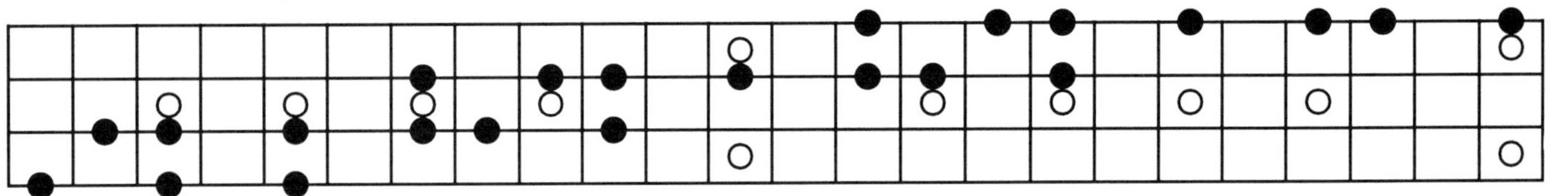

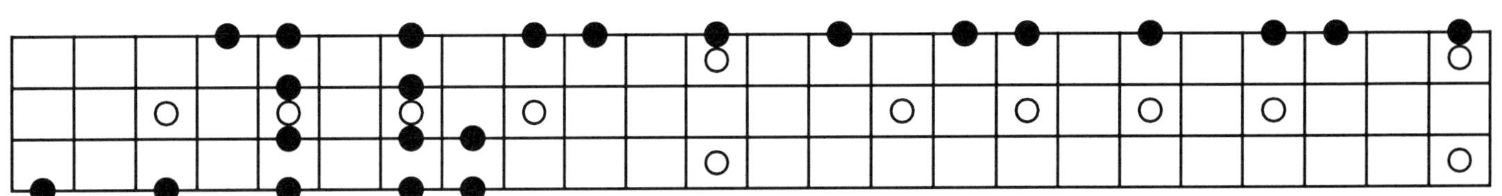

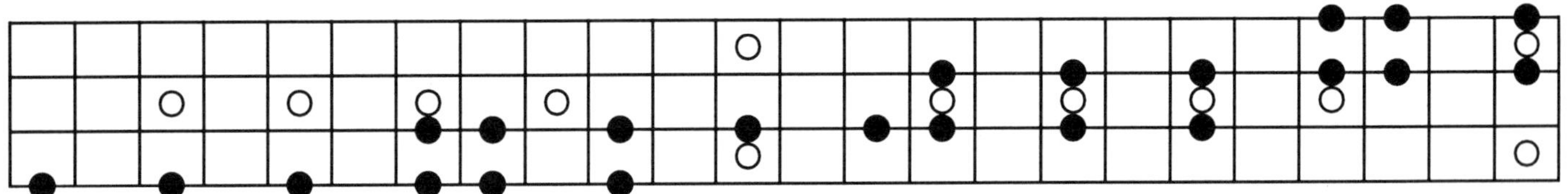